Growling at the Gentry

A Sharp Investigations Novel
Book Five
BY: E. N. CRANE
EDITED BY: A. O. NEAL &
SUE SCOTT

Dedication

Thank you to my dogs: Perry and Padfoot. You run this organization better than I could.

Thank you to my husband for bringing me snacks and coffee and my mom / editor for living in this world with me.

Most of all, thank you to the readers who keep joining Cyn and Winnie on their adventures and never once questioning my sanity. You are the real heros... and weirdos. Thank you for being my people.

Chapter One: Furry Situation

"For the love of dog, STOP!" I shouted, pumping my legs faster.

The olive drab cotton shirt I was wearing was stained with more condiments than even I could name, and the smears over my sweat outlined boobs smelled alarmingly like manure.

Though that could have been my pants... or my shoes.

Possibly the house itself.

Sweat dripped down my face, stinging my eyes but I didn't dare wipe it off or blink. If I blinked, I'd lose the little gremlin. If I wiped my face off, whatever was on my sleeve would end up on my face. Between days at the farm and nights spent babysitting, my entire world was a foul-smelling rollercoaster of physical endurance and psychological warfare.

"I'm serious!" I shouted again, but my niece cackled as she ran through the house. We'd started in the kitchen, cut through the dining room, and she had just thwarted my plan of corralling her in the downstairs bathroom. The little demon was now charging toward the living room and I couldn't fathom what would happen if she got away with her stolen goods.

Clutched in her hand was a bright orange square of cheese, and behind her was Winnie.

Sgt. Winnifred Pupperson, Army canine retired, was a lactose intolerant German shepherd-Malinois mix. Also known as Winnie, her love of cheese was rivaled only by my love of breathing without noxious gas asphyxiation. My niece, Sylvia... was a jerk who liked to steal my fresh air.

For an eight-year-old, she had a well-developed sense of violence and warfare. In the 1990s, they would have blamed video games or rock music by the likes of Marilyn Manson. In the early 2000's, they'd have blamed the parents and the decline of the nuclear family. As the century progressed though, it was more likely the result of either over-exposure to influencers on the Internet or a genetic predisposition to unleash chaos upon the world.

Considering my military career of destruction, it was probably genetics.

Coupled with my parents' penchant for public fornication and bondage, it could have come from either side of our family tree; and while my brother Seth's deceased wife was a saint, none of her personality traits were passed on to Sylvia.

The little clone of her mom served as a reminder that looks are often misleading.

"If you don't stuff that cheese in your mouth and sit down right now..." I started, but my toe caught on an end table. On that table was a hideous lamp shaped like an elephant that began to topple. My hand shot out to grab it and connected with a frog figurine that went flying toward the wall. My hand grasped for the lamp, pulled on the cord and it tangled around my feet, sending all size sixteen, six feet of me crashing to the ground with the ceramic elephant lamp.

A lamp that had been plugged in.

The lightbulb shattered, sparks arcing across the filament and traveled back down into the lamp. I yanked the cord hoping it would kill the spark traveling the insulated wire. My plan failed, the current continued and arced to the outlet with a puff of smoke and the smell of burning hair... before plunging the whole house into darkness.

"Her tongue tickles, Aunt Cyn!" Sylvia shouted, as my former partner made the slobbery sounds of consumption.

Please let her be eating something else.

"I need to get more cheese!"

Of course it was the cheese, I thought, banging my head on the floor. *Could this night possibly get any worse?*

A reminder, really, to never ask that question. It was followed by the sound of my nephew Eric shouting and my niece threatening him with a peanut butter facial.

Winnie's claws clattered in the dark and I blew out a breath.

"You all suck," I muttered.

"Your daughter belongs in a zoo. If I take this money, I could go down for being a paid accomplice to a future serial killer," I said, passing my brother back the small stack of cash he'd paid me for risking life and limb so he and his wife could have a date night. "And I'd call social services over the fact that you gave your child a chainsaw, but I think you deserve to suffer for that poor choice all on your own. Also, I don't have a phone and yours is useless without power."

"What?" He stuffed the money in my pants and pinched my love handles like all jerk brothers are known to do. "I didn't give her a chainsaw."

His teasing would cost him, since I decided to keep it to pay for the extra therapy sessions I'd need after this.

Also, something in my pants smelled like garlic cow farts and I wasn't ready to touch them.

My pants, garlic, or cow farts.

"Well, you gave her something. She threatened Eric with it after stealing his noise canceling headphones when the peanut butter facial re-aligned Winnie to his side of the war. I wrestled the headphones back from her before he fell apart, but I had to promise her free rein to destroy a small village until she was ultimately brought down by Dogzilla's gas. It seemed fitting her own weapon would bring about her downfall, but I have to take that weapon home and I don't think you paid me enough for the amount of cheese she gave Winnie. I'm going to ask that all cheese be removed from your house if I'm ever tricked into coming back. Your lamp and frog are totaled, your house has no power, and I'm fairly certain you need to call one of those companies that cleans up houses where violent crimes have happened because there is crap on the floor I wouldn't touch without a hazmat suit and a respirator."

Seth shrugged while beside him Carla held in a laugh.

"That's kind of how it normally looks... and smells."

"Then I guess there's no point in telling you about the sink-hole or the toilet. Eric needs new batteries in his headphones and a sensory deprivation chamber if you aren't shipping the terror off to Neverland," I added the last with a pang of guilt that I had zero control over his sister. My niece and nephew are unique and special in their own way, but my autistic nephew deserved better than being a second-class citizen to the madness that was Sylvia. For the most part, he played quietly and did his own thing, only asking for stuff to be kept at a low volume and not to be physically crowded.

In an act of unprecedented cruelty, the universe gave their family Sylvia.

With Sylvia around, there was no quiet, personal space, or cleanliness.

Especially since she discovered Daniel Kirby's kids had access to fireworks. One friendship led to another and now Sylvia was headed down the express lane to fugitive incarceration. My mom insists she's a "free spirit" and just needs to "work through it".

I'm fairly certain the only way to save mankind is to send her to a deserted island for reformation training by the world's top psychologists and behavioral experts. Like wherever they put Harley Quinn in Suicide Squad.

My mom said I was an exaggerating drama queen.

I told my mom that she'd regret that accusation when Sylvia succeeded in world domination and forced her to dance like a marionette puppet.

My mom threw a silicone dildo at my head and I declared her the official winner of our argument.

"Why do you have glow in the dark magic marker on your face?"

I swiped the back of my hand across my forehead and saw incandescent smears mixed with a chunky green fluid. My eyelids shut as I replayed the night's horrors in my mind. Some were already scheduled for traumatic memory suppression or whatever happened to Bing Bong in Inside Out.

I gagged when I remembered what had been on my sleeve that was now on my face.

"Uck, yeah. Eric decided to use my face as a distraction beacon. I'm leaving now... your house is a mess and your kids lost consciousness on the couch. Next time you need a night out, contact a prison warden," I started walking away as Carla gave up and burst out laughing. "If you ever ask me to do this again, I refuse to monitor your children in any place that isn't padded, surrounded by water with me on the other side, and devoid of sharp objects."

"If anyone in our family is there, there's always a Sharp object!" Seth shouted back and I offered him a stiff middle finger at the reminder of our last name. Opening the door, I climbed into my Jeep after Winnie. She leapt in gracelessly, clambered into the back, and flopped on her side, white belly exposed beside the tan and black fur. My entry wasn't much more graceful as I plopped into my seat and dropped my face on the steering wheel.

Two long inhales and exhales, and I felt my shoulders release some tension. At least enough that I could lift my head again. Around me, darkness covered everything in a veil of anonymity and I felt a calming silence settle in. It was the most peace I'd had in four hours and Winnie's light snore indicated she was spent right along with me.

But we'd survived and the horror was over. At least for tonight.

A second-floor window of my brother's house shattered and I heard Sylvia cackling.

"Oh my dog, she's escaped!" I shouted, turning over the engine and squealing the tires out of Seth's driveway. My Jeep zoomed down the street, revealing that my brother's house was the only one plunged into darkness on the block. I drove past house after house illuminated and spewing pajama clad residents onto their lawns to rubberneck a suspected murder in progress.

OK, so it was one neighbor and she was getting her mail, but it was only a matter of time before red and blue lights flooded this neighborhood.

Lost in thought, I came to a sudden stop when I realized I almost ran a stop sign. Pausing, I checked both directions and blinked at a movement in the shadows. It retained an almost alien shape as it moved with the speed of a sloth. Like a predator, my eyes tracked the figure, attempting to discern whether it was real or a trauma induced hallucination that would easily become an obsession if I started down the path, like children looking for the treasure at the end of the rainbow. Each movement swayed along with a stale breeze, a serpentine path over a deserted road by a... something.

Something big.

Something big that just fell over into the shrubs beside a white picket fence.

"Just go home, Cynthia," I whispered to myself as the figure staggered to upright, though potentially still hunched, and stumbled. My finger tapped on the steering wheel before flicking on the blinker. "Why aren't we going home?"

The car made a right turn and Winnie let out a loud snore from the back seat that sent my skin jumping after the total silence. Her claws clicked against each other, running in her sleep that was punctuated by a fart that rivaled air raid sirens in World War 2.

"Real smooth, girl. Now we..." The smell hit my nose and I gagged, choking and jerking the car until I slammed the brakes and came to a full stop. I threw my Jeep into park, and jumped out, dry heaving and gagging while my military working dog didn't so much as flutter an eyelid.

In front of my Jeep, the figure had frozen. It was roughly the size of a human adult, but on top of what would traditionally be the head were pointy protrusions that made the spiked arc of a regal crown perched atop. My eyes tried to zero in on the outline and identify the shape as it staggered closer, my heart racing as I braced myself to choose between physical pain and olfactory assault.

"Hey!" A muffled sound came from the approaching monster and I crouched low in anticipation of a tackle. "Help!"

My ears twitched, waiting for the figure to move into the pools of light created by the Jeep's Pelican headlamps. My breath stopped as first a furry black stick stepped in.

Next was a leg.

Then the whole figure toppled forward to reveal...

"Are you... wearing a cat costume?" I asked, relaxing and striding forward. The figure had landed on its face and I gracelessly hauled it to its feet.

While the nose looked a little dented from the fall, the rest of the outfit was a loose-fitting fur suit in black with white patches on the gloves and chest portion. Mesh green eyes let out the scent of alcohol and another plea for help.

"The clip is stuck and I can't get out!" The voice was male, but not very deep. Cautiously, I tilted up the cat head and saw a bicycle helmet clip securely fastened under a jaw with a few bristly hairs. I took a breath and yanked my face back.

"Holy cow, how much have you had to drink? And how did you drink it"

"Straws and a lot. I need to pee and maybe throw up. But I sewed the paws as part of the suit and I can't take them off to operate the buckle," I studied the arms of the cat suit and didn't see any gapping or seams to indicate they can be removed.

9

"Fine, hold your breath," I ordered the cat while following my own advice. Against all better judgment, I stuck my hands in the cat head and grasped for the plastic buckle I'd seen. It took a minute to press the release, a slippery sheen of sweat coating the clip and the strap around it.

At least I told myself it was sweat after the vomit warning I'd been given.

He did not smell like the vomit was a "maybe".

Once it was released, the cat threw off his head and heaved, vomiting all over my pants and shoes with an alcohol content that could peel paint. At the same time, I saw him clench his thighs together, either because he was peeing or trying desperately not to.

He should have tried harder with the vomit.

A long sigh escaped, but I carefully inhaled through my mouth as I watched the cat hunch on the side of the road. After two more heaves, it staggered upright and swayed back to me.

"Sorry," he mumbled. Acne scarred skin and bright blue eyes rimmed in red blood-shot vessels blinked at me. "I need more help."

He turned his back and showed me a fluffy tail. Furry paws grasped at a seam, peeling Velcro that immediately stuck to his paws.

"Take off my clothes."

"Shouldn't I buy you dinner first?" I asked, taking a step back when he heaved again.

"Please don't mention food." He swiped at his mouth with a paw and I grimaced at the smeared bile on the costume fur's white patch.

"Right.... Turn around and hold your breath."

He followed my instructions and I yanked apart the Velcro to get to the plastic zipper. He exhaled painfully and I realized that drunk and barfing was ill-suited to breath holding. He could only manage for so long and I was taking more time than he had. My fingers shook in horror as I slowly lowered the zipper and tried to move my face as far from him as possible.

"Oh my dog, you're naked!" I screamed and jumped away. With enough of the zipper down, he pulled apart the rest and the costume pooled at the base of his eerily thin frame. Unlike part of my face, his skin didn't quite glow in the dark but he wasn't wearing magic marker. The exposed flesh of his butt cheeks reflected my headlights in a display that would make Bart Simpson proud and reminded me that someone made a song about wearing sunglasses at night.

"Oh thank god," he staggered to the side of the road, taking with him the costume puddled around his ankles. He stopped by a fence post, leaned against it, and let loose a stream of urine so long and loud, it woke Winnie up and she pressed her nose to the glass to watch.

"Right... I'm gonna..." I gestured to my car, still impressed by the steadily growing puddle at his feet. If I didn't work on a farm, this might have been the most urine I'd seen come from a living creature and I felt the urge to hold up a scorecard with the number nine.

"Wait!" He held a finger above his head, even as the puddle threatened to get onto his cat costume. "I need to get back to the party."

"I think you need to go home and go to bed," I countered, slowly backing away. He turned suddenly, giving me a full frontal and a clear view of his swinging junk.

Like a freeway car wreck, I couldn't look away from the wrinkled flesh of his manhood.

"I can't! My pants are at the party."

His voice was coming from his face, but I couldn't bring myself to meet his gaze.

"Do you only own one pair of pants? Can't you forfeit them? Submit a request that they be sold to benefit an organization that... neuters cats?"

"No... My keys are in there. And my wallet... and..." he trailed off when he noticed I was still staring at his one-eyed snake. "A condom?"

My eyes snapped up and I choked on my spit.

"What? No, I have a boyfriend. I'm just terrified that if I look away it will get fluids on me like your mouth did! How did so much urine come out of... that?" My face burned and he shrugged, pulling the costume completely off and bundling it into his cat head.

"Mr. Wiggles has a lot of skills... Your boyfriend must not be very good if you're shopping around and Mr. Wiggles is available," he smirked.

"You named your penis Mr. Wiggles and speak about it in the third person?"

"Yeah. Wanna know what I'd name your tits?" He wiggled his eyebrows and I wanted to choose violence.

Wanted to but didn't.

Not for the moral high ground but for the crucial life goal of never touching him.

"Larry is perfectly suited to fulfill my-"

"Larry? Larry Kirby?" He interrupted and I nodded. His eyes were unfocused, and a small stream of drool was slipping out of his mouth, but he apparently knew there was only one Larry in Sweet Pea.

"I was going to swing by his house and say goodnight before heading home. So I don't need-"

"Perfect, you can drop me off," he swayed and staggered toward the passenger side door. Winnie scented the air and just as he gripped the handle, she let out a whimper. Her body disappeared into the back seat as the naked man placed his uncovered junk on my cloth seats.

At a loss, I went to the driver's side door and yanked it open.

He was rubbing his naked butt on the upholstery trying to get comfortable, really grinding in that naked man scent.

"Where am I dropping you off?" I grumbled, hoping it wasn't far. Between the grime on my outfit and the fluids on his cat costume, my car was going to need sage, bleach, and possibly an autoclave to ever feel clean again.

"Larry's house. That's where Amber's party is."

Chapter Two: The Break-Up

C at Man hadn't been wrong.

Sweet Pea, Ohio was a twenty-horse town with thirty-eight light poles and more livestock than human residents. It was thirty minutes from Yellow Springs, an hour from Dayton, and just a small notch above homo erectus in terms of intellectual evolution. Since coming back here, I've been invited to more monster truck rallies and pig races than I thought could be held in an eight month period.

Yet, here I was, well aware the squealing piglets do not run in a straight line.

Following Cat Man's directions, my stomach sunk lower and lower when he led me down the familiar route to my boyfriend's house. While Larry may not be an uncommon name, I had hoped that he'd been confused and the party was at Daniel Kirby's house. Or maybe Cat Man thought I'd said Gary or Jerry.

Unlike our many Earls, any one of those names could live in town.

The music could be heard as soon as I turned on Main Street. Saturday night at Casey's Bar was loud, but it was nothing compared to the thumping beat of techno two streets down and one over. Casey's Bar was set up like an old west saloon and traditionally played classic rock, country and whatever ABBA is, but never techno and people generally walked there. Cars overflowed the quiet street, bleeding out to the main drag in a volume a medical professional would term hemorrhage.

Or someone recently vomited on by a drunk man in a cat costume would consider...

A really bad night.

After circling twice and finding every lot on Main St. filled, I illegally double parked behind Mary's Muffins and More. Since the owner Mary O'Connor, also known as Mo, is my best human friend, it seemed like a safe place to break the law and it was within viewing distance of my destination.

Also, it was her car I was blocking in and if it was parked here at this hour, it was probably done moving for at least the next hour.

Or at least that's what I thought until I saw her curly red hair staggering toward me. Her hair was attached to a body clad in a skimpy fox outfit held up by a figure I recognized as Chris. Chris was Mo's firefighter/EMT boyfriend she met when I shot off a man's hand in the bakery behind us. He also worked as a nurse, and despite my regular need for medical attention, he refused to offer his services to me. Since I'd seen a naked picture of him during a rash of murder and blackmail, I was well aware of what "services" he offered Mo.

It was not those services I needed, however. Nope, I wanted him when my butt needed stitches after an incident with barbed wire... and last month's incident with alcohol, gravity, and an unfortunately placed rusty nail.

But *noooo*, seeing his friend's naked bloody butt would be "weird".

Frankly, where the man drew his lines should be the subject of a doctoral thesis on controlled psychosis.

Luckily, the emergency room was like a second home to me and I was this close to having my own coffee mug there. Like Tim Allen on the sitcom from the nineties, except I had fewer concussions and no definitive knowledge of cars. My presence was generally accepted in emergency rooms, and stories of my injuries were often accompanied with YouTube videos, pre-loaded for ready display and mockery. Unlike Sylvia's chemical and auditory warfare, my disasters have mostly happy endings... except maybe the cow in Sweden and my failure to demolish all of Florida.

I still insist that the cow's death was an accident.

As far as Florida, if I ever returned, I'd try harder.

At least the exploding fuel yard and brush fire were a good start.

"Mo! What the hell?" I demanded and she removed her face from Chris's neck to look at me. In its place were hickeys, smeared lipstick, and... blood? "Did you know about this?"

I decided not to comment on the rest of my observations.

"Cyn! Are you here for the party? Daniel is shutting it down in a minute after... why the hell is there a naked guy passed out in your Jeep?"

I glanced behind me and saw that Cat Man had indeed passed out. From this angle though, you could hardly tell he was naked. It was also impossible to know if it was his or Winnie's snores vibrating the car.

My Jeep's fate was in limbo... or it was until an explosion of Winnie gas ripped through the night. The vehicle beside Mo's started to alarm and an approaching Alligator Man beeped the remote in his hand, high-fived Chris, and then threw up in the planter before staggering further up the alley.

I raised a questioning brow but Chris just shrugged and I looked back at Mo, staring expectantly in my direction.

"Sorry, what?" I asked, still confused if Alligator Man was headed for the sewers or if Casey's bar was getting an influx of animal themed patrons.

"The naked man, Cyn!"

"Right. Long story... Why are you dressed like a fox? Why is Chris..." I glanced up and down his muscular frame and tilted my head. He had crisscross leather straps on his chest and cowhide chaps over skin tight fleece leggings.

"I'm a Bucentaur," he claimed, wrapping his arms around Mo's waist. He then needed to take custody of her hands to get them out of his fleece leggings that were looking a little tight in his manly region the more she rubbed against him.

"Whatever that is, I don't want to see your penis in real life. Mo, hands to yourself! What is going on over there?" I asked, watching red and blue lights flood the street and a sea of scantily clad and full suit animals pour out of Larry's front door. A good quarter of them were being held up by another quarter of the animals, leaving half to swerve and manage on their own. "Cat Man said it's Amber's party."

"Cat Man?" Mo asked, only to be answered by the door of my Jeep opening and the strangled sounds of a man vomiting up the empty contents of his stomach.

"He was dressed as a cat before he was naked," I clarified and she narrowed her eyes for a better look. My passenger door slammed shut and he wandered over with his costume under one arm and his whole body proudly on display.

"Hey," he waved at Mo and Chris before walking upstream of the evacuating animals toward Larry's house. Mo watched his pale butt reflect the moonlight before a musical giggle slipped from her throat.

"With the full moon, you need to be a werewolf, Cyn!" Her giggle turned into a cackle and Chris covered her mouth as a passing frog flinched and slapped his flippers over the green painted human ears he hadn't incorporated into the outfit.

"Nighttime voice, babe."

She smiled at him with gooey marshmallow eyes and I fought the urge to squirm and look away.

Cute couple things were absolutely beyond my comfort level. Watching them was the most uncomfortable I've been all night even though there had been a naked man in my Jeep *and* I had vomit on my pants.

"Back to the 'party'," I hooked finger quotes around the word party because I had doubts. While the music and intoxication levels of the attendees offered reasonable evidence to the word, every outfit suggested "orgy" would have been more accurate.

Give me a black light and I'd be able to prove it.

"Did Larry tell you about it?"

"No. Larry wasn't there when it started... and I'm not completely sure who I saw come in when it was ending. I'm part of a group who's really into animal play. Nothing weird... well, a little kinky, but that's all..." I held up a hand and gestured for her to skip ahead. "Right, so I saw on a message board that there was going to be a fur pile. Do you know what a fur pile is?"

I nodded my head, remembering an unfortunate incident when I was 18. I heard about a Furry Party and thought it was for animal lovers.

In a way I was right.

In a lot of ways, I was very wrong.

Not that I left before experiencing the spectacle.

Or getting questionable stains on my clothing that my mom reminds me of every time I express concern over her hobbies.

When I call them her "hobbies" she says it's a lifestyle and I need a bit more kink in mine.

I pulled out a crimping iron and she smacked me on the side.

My mom was declared the official winner of that argument.

"Great! So, I signed up for updates and when I got the address, it was Larry's. I thought maybe the two of you were getting more adventurous but then neither of you was there. Where is Larry?" She looked around again, as though noticing for the first time that a second drunk and naked guy hadn't stumbled from my car.

"Not sure. I haven't talked to him today. You thought you saw him?"

My eyes were glued on the front of the house. The outpouring of animals had slowed to a trickle.

"Maybe? Someone came in shouting, kicked everyone out of the bedroom, slammed the door and then ten minutes later, Daniel showed up. Why? Are you guys fighting?" Chris asked, face scrunched in either concern or he was experiencing gas.

Since he was half-cow I decided to hold my breath in case there was methane.

After spluttering and choking on my own spit, I declared the air methane free.

"Not that I know of. I lost my phone." I shrugged, hoping no one asked for details. *Lost* was a kindness that my phone would not have appreciated being used to describe how it got covered in after birth and trampled by goats before meeting its final resting place in the remnants of a tub of dark chocolate cherry ice cream. "Was Amber there?"

Mo pressed her lips together and a sinking feeling filled my stomach. Amber Carter was my childhood bully and that hadn't changed when she continued to feel the need to belittle me as an adult. She was also the most obnoxious adult with narcissistic personality disorder that hadn't managed to run for president. She had more money than sense, an air of entitlement rivaling a former president, and a disappearing criminal record to match.

"Promise you won't freak out? I think she went into Larry's room when Daniel showed up..." Mo paled as I felt my anger flame through my face. I shook my head before declaring a state of emergency and moving past them with an internal war cry. "Cyn! Don't!"

I ignored Mo's shouts and sprinted toward the adjacent corner. My toe caught on the curb, but I caught myself and carried on storming the castle. At the walkway, Daniel was standing sentry on the porch holding his breath. I started to shove past him when the smell caught in my nose and I gagged.

"What the hell? Did your sister-in-law send you to check up on me?" The deputy was in half of his uniform.

As a repayment for my suffering, the universe made it the bottom half.

With a lighter than normal duty belt.

"No. Where the hell is your shirt? And your gun?" I asked, trying to breathe through my mouth. Watching Daniel wince, I followed his gaze to a group of men over my shoulder. Turning fully, I saw a lot of frosted tips, defined muscle, and spandex before whipping back around.

"They stole it and rubbed it against their..." he gestured to my crotch area with his eyes. "Not over the clothes either."

"Your shirt or the gun?" I gaped at them again and watched one in a thong quick draw on his buddy in pasties. "Oh my dog, seriously? Both?"

"Please don't tell Chief Sharp. I managed to eject the magazine as they took it and I don't carry one in the chamber because... well you've met my kids. It's completely safe." His eyes pleaded as he begged me not to send him on a one-way ride to the unemployment office. When I heard the gun click empty, I sighed in relief and considered the man before me. Smiling smugly, I considered all the ways to leverage this new information with my new sister-in-law who was also his boss.

"What's in it for me?" I asked, crossing my arms and then yanking them back again. "Oh dog!"

Another gag escaped and I doubled over. Encountering vomit, I righted myself and tried to cover my nose with my sleeve. It still smelled like playdough, garlic, and manure and I had to fight another gag to get it safely away from my face. My sleeves were glowing in the dim light and I stared in horror at that glow coming from the bottom half of my left leg.

There was a black light out here.

There was a black light and I had a fluid stain... a really big fluid stain.

"What's on your pants?" Daniel looked as appalled as I was.

"I'm not sure. Do you think it's worse that I don't know what it is or that I'm not surprised it's on me?"

He snickered and another wave of the stench from Larry's living room mingled with my own funk and I dry-heaved over the lawn.

"Yeah... it's nasty in there," he misinterpreted my disgust. "Amber is quite the hostess."

My eyes narrowed into slits as I whipped toward him again. The nausea was now twice what it had been but my eyes flashed violence at Daniel. His predicament had temporarily interrupted my crusade and now I remembered.

Amber... Amber had invaded my boyfriend's house and I had no idea where he was.

"Amber? So, Amber threw this party?"

"That's what I gather. She's with Larry in his room if you want more info, but I gotta warn you..."

None of his words registered as I shoved him aside and stormed into the house. Just inside was the living room, couch flipped over and food particles crushed into the carpet. To the left was the kitchen, a sea of glass bottles and plastic cups propped on flipped over barstools. Beyond was the dining room where I once found a severed finger in a jar.

It was still less disturbing than this.

Beside the food and booze were furry costume pieces. Tails, ears, and paw shaped gloves mingled with congealed globs I refused to identify. A grunt came from Larry's bedroom and I shoved open the door to see a woman's thong covered ass straddling a man's legs.

A tail attached to the T was striped like a raccoon, and when the head popped up, I saw matching ears and messy brown hair.

"Amber?"

She flipped her hair over a shoulder to give me a victorious grin.

Her eyes dripped with venom and spite, but her nasally voice remained silent. Beneath her, the even breath of her victim.

Almost like he'd been asleep.

Or passed out.

I inched in closer as she turned back and pressed her mouth against the form beneath her, grinding her lady parts against the man's package. He muttered nonsense as his hands fought themselves free of her legs to press roughly against her barely clothed chest.

"Stop, Amber." A male voice came from beneath her just as I came around to where the man's head lay, propped on pillows. "I said no."

His hands remained on her breasts as a sharp pain stabbed through my chest. The brown-haired man beneath her looked to massage the soft tissue as I fought back a gag and she continued rubbing herself against him.

"Larry?" I whispered and his eyes snapped to me.

"Cyn! Where the hell have you been? I've been calling you all night." He tried to push Amber off, but she locked her legs at his waist. "Let me up, Amber!"

"I mean, you were up earlier, but I can start again," she sneered at me as her hips gyrated against Larry. His face went red, his hands grabbing her hips to move her, giving the look of two people in the throes of passion and I fought back tears.

"Cyn! It's not what it looks like!" He freed himself, struggling to his feet with unzipped pants and no shirt on. His rumpled hair and bare feet were all the proof I needed. "All I wanted to do was come home and sleep. My mom gave her the key, I was just..."

I shoved my fist into his face with all the force I possessed, hearing the satisfying crunch of his nose beneath my knuckles, before I spun around and ran.

Chapter Three:
Half-Baked

"What are you doing?" My mom winced at her own volume and cleared her throat to try again. "It's one in the morning, Cynthia. How did you get in here?"

"Key," I whispered, though it was unclear if she heard me. Any other day I'd remind her that I lived here for eighteen years and she'd never demanded I return any of the two dozen keys that I'd needed to have made over the years.

To be fair, there was only one of those keys remaining in usable condition but I hadn't lost it... yet.

Lynn Sharp was wearing a tattered bathrobe and furry slippers. Her normally perfect hair was mussed from sleep, her frame looking much larger than it was due to her small stature. Though my dad was the cook in the house, my mom ruled the kitchen.

She determined where everything was stored and no one was permitted to re-arrange her kitchen or the rest of the house. My dad even consulted her before putting his underwear away to make sure she would approve.

Personal preservation kept me from asking if it was part of her Dom/sub relationship with my dad. Though as far as I know, that relationship dynamic was far newer than her iron clad rule over the house, residents and property held within.

Except me... and Winnie.

The Army wasn't the first regime we failed to fall in line with and compared to my mom, they were significantly easier to ignore.

"What have you done to my kitchen?"

My eyes burned from tears as I looked around her kitchen.

Every surface was covered in flour, dough and freshly baked pastries. To my left was the snickerdoodle cookies I'd started with, only half remaining as I ate my feelings. Adjacent to that was the pie station, rolled and cut dough pressed into the glass pans beside a pumpkin pie in a ready-made crust while I'd cut butter into the cooled pie dough and searched for corn syrup to make pecan pie.

Half the pumpkin pie was gone as well and despite having a full stomach, I felt empty and stuffed another three cookies in my mouth. Immediately forgetting the cookies, I opened my mouth to explain. Explain the vomit on my pants even though I'd showered and changed after my babysitting gig, when I forced more food into my stomach than it wanted or needed. Tell her how I'd cleaned out every baking supply at the corner market that was also a gas station and raided her house three hours ago to relieve the agony in my heart with sugar and edible chemistry.

The first half of which I'd thrown up in her trashcan but I couldn't stop eating.

In my mind I told her about Larry. About needing to bake to take the edge off my pain and eat my feelings, but all that came out was a strangled sound mutated with mucus into something that belonged coming from a creature on the Wookie planet.

When I tried again, the words turned into a sob and I collapsed onto my knees in the middle of the kitchen.

"Cynthia?" My mom's voice took on a softer edge, pushing me over the edge again. Tears spilled from my eyes, fat droplets running down my cheeks and bringing the taste of flour into my mouth. I just shook my head, hoping to shake the images from my head.

Amber.

Half-naked Amber on top of Larry.

Kissing him... rubbing herself against him... after wrecking his house having a party.

Together.

My mom was on the ground beside me, questions in her eyes that she knew not to ask. She pulled me into a hug, and I collapsed against her to sob. We stayed on the floor, her hands running through my hair as I shook with sobs until my body gave up and went deathly still.

"It's going to be alright, sweetie. Whatever it is, it's going to be alright," she whispered into my shoulder and I couldn't help but feel like she was wrong when I grabbed her trashcan and threw up the cookies.

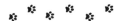

There was no light when I opened my eyes, and I thought maybe I'd died.

A painful scratch in my throat dismissed the notion almost immediately. If I'd died, the number of times I'd thrown up and the excessively hot cookies I'd eaten would no longer be an issue. A scrape of claws against my arm was accompanied by the audible *pooft* of air escaping a small opening and a stench that threatened to end my life where yesterday's events had failed.

"Seriously, Winnie! Is it too much to hope for a peaceful death?" I croaked out. Around me, the air moved and the stench surrounded me completely with every wag of her tail. "Oh my dog!"

I choked on a gag and stood to run.

Sadly, it was too dark to notice the wooden laundry bag immediately by the foot of the bed. K

My toe caught, I let out a scream and crashed to the floor. The heavy weight of a dog landed on my back, her wet tongue swiping my neck just before another earth-shaking fart escaped her butt and she jumped off to do a dance of victory and I curled into myself, grabbing my foot. A warm sensation bloomed over my second toe, and I knew even in the dark that I was bleeding.

"What else you got, universe?" I shouted in the direction of the ceiling, a small part of me cracking alongside my damaged voice. "Are you going to tell me that there's no such thing as ducklings? That rainbows are just a hallucinogenic flashback to drugs I never took? Or are you going to tell me that there will never be anymore puppies, ever and the most pure species has run its course? That unicorns and dragons only exist on the blacklight posters of drug addicts?"

Light flooded the room and I winced, tucking my face under my arm.

"Great! Now you shine light on my suffering. Fluff off universe!"

"Cynthia?" My mom asked and I whimpered into my arm that I was mostly alive.

"Cynthia... I..." She broke off and a new voice penetrated my pounding head.

"Cyn, we need..." my eyes snapped up to glare at Larry. His eyes had deep purple bruising under them, a plastic strip crossing the bridge of his nose over a slight gash. The sight sent a painful jab of something that felt like guilt and bitter satisfaction had a baby.

One that forced acid up my throat behind my sternum.

Dehydrated and fresh off a sugar hangover, I wanted water and a vegetable. I did not want to rip open my newly cauterized metaphorical wounds and leak emotions like the blood coating my toe. I didn't want him to see the effect he had on me.

And I really didn't want to feel bad for hitting him.

"Go away," I growled, Winnie's back fluff rising in an imitation of a stegosaurus. "Go away or lose an appendage."

Winnie growled beside me, and Larry looked scared for the first time since meeting Winnie ten months ago. Every wave of anger and hurt that rolled off me sent her fur higher and higher along her back until it was nearly vertical coming out of her skin. The veterinarian wisely retreated when both our lips curled back and offered a glimpse of our sharpest teeth with the next snarl.

"Could you both just calm down..." he started and before I could command Winnie to attack, my mom sent an elbow into his gut that forced him to fold into himself.

"Don't tell them to calm down. Don't tell any woman to calm down Lawrence. Actually, don't tell any woman anything. Your speaking privileges are revoked. March yourself to the kitchen, make my daughter a cup of coffee and stay there until someone tells you you're allowed to move," her clipped voice offered no room for argument, and I nearly applauded when he hung his head and obeyed without a word.

Maybe she was onto something with that whole Dom thing.

"Thanks ma," I whispered, and she offered a curt nod of her sharp blonde bob before descending into the basement and into the ensuite bathroom. Cabinets opened and closed, water ran briefly, and I stared up at my best friend, tracing circles on Winnie's triangle shaped ears.

"I need you to sit on the bed," she crouched in front of me and I followed her instructions. The damp red washcloth, cotton balls and brown bottle of hydrogen peroxide speaking for itself. After wiping off the excess blood, she applied the disinfectant with a cotton swab and gave me a long look when I didn't wince at the subtle sting.

"When you were little, this used to make you cry," she spoke softly, studying my face. "When did that change?"

I blinked at her, head tilting.

"I grew up, ma," I said, watching her hands wrap my toe in a band aid. "I grew up and... well... you've seen me walk down a street..."

A small smile graced her lips.

"Your lack of coordination, like your height, comes from your father. You two are far more similar than I'd like to admit," a look crossed her face so quickly that I questioned if I'd imagined it. "Except your father can follow instructions. Your sisters all got my stubborn, to hell with them attitude. You and Seth... you two were always a bit more sensitive. I tried to help you fight back, but I think it just came off as more bullying."

"No, ma. It wasn't you. I can't speak for Seth, but when you are already the class's Jolly Blonde Giant, the last thing you want is to tell people off and be accused of bullying 'the little people'. It was easier just to hold it in and let it go, letting it out would have just caused more trouble." I squeezed her hand on the bed beside me and tried not to squirm when tears sparkled in her eyes. "Please... don't cry. I'm sorry. I'll... punch Larry again?"

She cackled and swiped at her face.

"That was you?"

"Yeah..." I studied my knuckles. They were only slightly bruised, and I was forced to admit my hand had grown unnaturally accustomed to punching people in the face. "Kinda wanna hit him again so your permission would be appreciated but I think my medical insurance is on the verge of being canceled."

I hauled myself to standing and offered my mom a hand. Fully erect, she barely made it to my boobs but I still felt small standing next to her.

"If he says something stupid, go for it. I'll figure out how to get you back on my policy," she said, taking my hand and leading me up the stairs in my pajamas and bandaged toe. "Though I'd prefer if you intend to make him bleed, you do it outside. The patio is very easy to hose down and this carpet is somewhat new."

We emerged at the top of the stairs and her eyes zeroed in on Larry sitting at the kitchen table.

"I also don't want him forensically linked to this house in the event of his sudden and questionable death."

His face lost a shade of color beneath the bruising and my mom nodded once to confirm her intention before turning to face me.

"I'm going upstairs to punish your father. The neighbors will not be alarmed by any additional screaming but please do not interrupt, I've been forcing him to deny himself release for two days and it's extremely painful for both of us." She pressed a kiss to my cheek on tip toes and I shuddered. "Really, Cynthia. That was practically clinical."

With a shake of her head, she disappeared to the second floor and left me alone with the man I had been dating. A man I loved and almost considered spending forever with right after I got over the Army induced fear of legally binding contracts. At the end of the day, he was just a man. Weak, impulse driven and destructive.

I didn't need him.

"I'm fine alone," I spoke only to myself.

A whimper sounded and I looked down at Winnie.

Not alone.

With Winnie, I was never alone.

"Sorry girl. We'll be OK," I breathed the words and she bumped her head against my hand in acknowledgement. I rubbed her ears and took a deep breath.

Ignoring Larry for the moment, I went into the kitchen and picked up a filled and sweetened mug of coffee and took a long drink. The cup he'd chosen was a deep fishbowl size with a plain metallic shimmer that would never have been permitted in my house.

Apparently, my mom's taste in coffee cups was less snark and sparkle.

But sparkle wasn't microwave safe and I was not known for making good decisions when it came to coffee.

Cup half empty, I searched the kitchen for two bowls and the dog food my mom kept on hand for Winnie. Finishing the other half of my coffee, I studied the cabinet dedicated to Winnie. It was filled with the food, bowls, treats and dog toys she has despite "not wanting that dog in her house".

Apparently, my mom is a softie.

Winnie food and water bowls filled, I moved around an exuberant Winnie to place her bowls on the far end of the kitchen island. Her crunching chomps filled the kitchen, and I poured another cup of coffee from the now half-empty pot as smooth jazz filtered from the upstairs bedroom. The music had a heavy bass that I imagine was chosen to cover up any... impacts.

I shuddered and shared a glance with Winnie.

She was totally judging my hypocrisy while her eyebrows danced.

"I'm not being a hypocrite. It's always weird to know when your parents are getting jiggy with it!" Her eyebrows danced with a partial glance toward the dining room. "He's not your dad and you didn't come out of me!"

A male throat cleared, forcing my eyes to the doorway of the kitchen. Larry was leaning on the jam, arms and ankles crossed with a small smile playing at his lips. My chest ached at his scruffy, casual appearance and I had to clasp my hands together to avoid reaching out to touch him.

When did I become so obsessed with touching him?

"I'm kind of her dad," he smirked, and I let out a growl that Winnie echoed even as I felt warm and fuzzy at his feelings toward my best friend.

"No one returned your speaking privileges, Lawrence Kirby," I snapped, and he uncrossed his arms, holding them in front of him defensively. He looked more than a little upset but I was well and truly past upset so it was his job to just suck it up.

Which brought back images of Amber on his face.

"I get that last night..." I cut him off with another growl and something heavy thudded against the floor above us.

Another slam and Winnie tucked her tail, prepared to run.

"Yeah... I'm with you girl. Backyard, doctor," I gestured toward the slider off the dining room and followed him out of the kitchen, grabbing Winnie's bowls so she could dine al fresco in the fresh soon to be fall air.

We got to the concrete slab that served as a patio, and I set down Winnie's dishes. The backyard hadn't changed much since I was little. There was grass over most of the quarter acre yard with a stone path leading to an aging storage shed that used to house garden tools and spiders.

Now my parents paid a landscaper and used it as a second adult playroom.

I was too scared to go inside and see if there were still any spiders.

The concrete patio had a slatted awning and two patio chairs, but I couldn't bring myself to sit with Larry. Instead, I crouched beside Winnie before sitting cross-legged and staring at my naked feet. They were large, slightly brown from walking barefoot outside, with fading glitter green nail polish from a drunken girl's night at Mo's.

We remained silent for a few moments as Winnie chomped and a gentle breeze ruffled the plants along the fence line. Larry's scent didn't carry on the breeze and I wondered if it would be comforting or agonizing. If I reached for him, would he hold me or flinch away?

"Should I start?" Larry asked, settling himself on the ground facing me. His face was soft, and if it weren't for my personal knowledge of events, I'd say he looked hurt.

Instead of answering, I shrugged and picked at the polish on my pinkie toe.

"Last night wasn't my idea. It was planned and executed completely without me. I had no idea there was a party at my house until my neighbors called and complained. You know I was out of town yesterday tending to an injured mare, and I was hauled back out midday for another one. Something is spooking the horses out off of Brave Heart Trail, and this is the third one who's been hurt running from whatever that something is. After trying and failing to spot a predator, werewolf, Chupacabra or illegal fireworks, I threw in the towel and went home to address the chaos. I texted you all of this, but you never answered. You didn't answer my calls, my texts and when I knocked on the door to your apartment, you didn't answer that either. I was pissed when I stomped into my house, kicked everyone out of my room and called my brother. I tried calling your mom, but she didn't know where you were. Carla and Seth weren't picking up... it was like your whole family ghosted me. You weren't even mad that I was leaving town and suddenly you were ignoring me. Why were you ignoring me?"

"I lost my phone at work yesterday and then I was child-sitting my niece and nephew," I shrugged, feeling part of me warm to him while the other brought up the image of Amber riding him.

Kissing him.

Reminding me that his body had reacted to her presence.

And now I was pissed again.

"That doesn't change anything, Larry. Even if you didn't know I lost my phone, that doesn't erase what I saw. One day without talking to me you're grinding one out against Amber Carter?"

"I wasn't grinding one out against her, she was grinding one out against me. It wasn't consensual!"

I scoffed and glared at him.

"You weren't trying very hard to get away."

"I was mostly asleep! She came into my bedroom while I was passed out!" His face was turning red, but I couldn't bring myself to care if he was angry or embarrassed.

"She came into your house with a key, Larry. How did she get a key?"

"I told you, my mom gave it to her!" He shoved his hands through his hair, wincing at the pressure against his injured face. "I didn't invite her. She told my mom she wanted to have a gathering in town and surprise me with a home cooked meal. When I confronted my mom this morning, she said she thought it meant you and I were finally done and I was moving on to something better."

Tears stung my eyes and I blinked them back. His mom... she thought I wasn't good enough. Despite her grandchildren's propensity toward a life of crime, my parent's behavior, her own behavior as a person interested in "horse play", I wasn't good enough.

"Well, I guess you're available for that then," I rose to my feet and collected Winnie's bowls as he stared at me. "I'm not fighting your mom, Larry. Not after this. She's proven time and again that she doesn't want us together and I can't keep pretending it doesn't bother me. That her looking down on me and my family while she has a stable to ride your father like a pony in the woods isn't the most hypocritical nonsense. If she'd rather you be with Amber, then I won't get in your way."

"What about what I want, Cyn?" He shouted, climbing to his feet and reaching for me, but Winnie let out a threatening rumble.

"It doesn't matter what you want, Larry. Your mom doesn't want us together and I'm not going to fight her for you. Not after last night," I remembered his hands stroking Amber's exposed breasts and shook my head. "I'm sure she'll grow on you like that thing in your pants did with her rubbing against it. After all, her dad has money and influence. All I have is an unhealthy attraction to explosions and a dog."

"Cyn!"

I shook my head.

"I'm fine with just the dog, Larry."

I went inside the sliding door, pausing to let Winnie get one last look, and locked it behind us.

Chapter Four: Desperation

There was no hope for my sanity in my mom's house.

I stayed there all of Sunday and now I had disturbing auditory clips to go with my emotional pain. Nothing like hearing wild west sounds punctuated with fleshy slapping while sobbing into a gallon of bubblegum ice cream.

Armed with four bags of coffee, three King Size peanut butter cups, a family sized bag of nacho cheese chips and three pounds of Goldfish crackers, I sat at the desk in my office and waited. My thoughts were not easy to drown out, even with the crunch of chips and the percolating coffee pot.

I needed something else.

I needed a disaster or a mystery of epic proportions to keep my compartmentalized feelings locked where they belonged. Buried deep and ignored for one to two years until I either suffered an aneurysm or could sign up for an experimental memory augmenting brain autopsy while still alive. There was no way I could deal with Larry's betrayal and continue to function as a human being.

Where are all the damn nut jobs? My brain asked, dumping the last of the pot I had made into my mug and watching the sun glint off my business name stuck to the window.

Sharp Investigations, my unpaid occupation that offered me a glimpse into the madness of others, was having a slow week. Normally, the office was crawling with potential murderers, ambitious arsonists, and victims of gravity and poor life choices. This week, however, it felt like the town had finally decided to use a Groupon for electroshock behavioral modification. Only one person had been in all week, and it was a woman who worked at the library informing me that the book I'd placed on hold was "accidentally" destroyed by Larry's mother and they were ordering another copy.

A fact that hadn't bothered me until today.

Today it was another example of her interfering in my life and relationships. Without either that book or an influx of visitors, things were looking a little too open for emotional processing. Just at this moment, I didn't need to process things. I needed something to steal the agonizing pain from my chest and it was too early for my best friend's alcohol and refined sugar.

Cheese, on the other hand, was just not cutting it.

"Should we turn to ambulance chasing?" I asked Winnie, watching her eyebrows dance on her forehead. "I know we hate running, but the exercise would be good for us. Larry said you were putting on weight…"

My eyes scrunched in annoyance at myself.

Nothing he said was relevant or important.

"Right. No one said anything. I need something to do, girl," I huffed, watching her drape a paw over her face. Apparently, my sadness was interrupting her nap. "It wouldn't hurt you to chase your ball or something to distract me."

I tossed the bright orange ball her way only to watch it bounce off her head. The ball rolled under my coffee cart and she stared blankly after it.

"Come on! Fetch!"

Winnie yawned and rolled onto her back in the canine equivalent of talk to the hand… Except she was more inclined to make me converse with her fluffy backside. It would have been insulting if her butt weren't so dang cute.

When Winnie and I had retired from the Army, she had quickly lost what little discipline the military had forced into her. She retained her knowledge and skills, but her willingness to protect and serve was limited to moments of danger and food acquisition. I had never managed more discipline than wearing the same outfit as everyone else, so it was perfectly reasonable we'd promptly become slovenly and unmotivated. Neither of us had any real business investigating and getting justice for our community. We were content as ordinary citizens until forced into an arms-dealing investigation linked to a not-quite-dead colonel, a fake reverend, and his daughter the criminal mastermind.

Now we had this swanky office, a tiny apartment above it, and an agreement with the town elders to help anyone who needed investigative skills and had little to no proof of a crime being perpetrated. Today, however, it offered zero distractions from the misery that had become my life.

"I should have taken up mercenary work... always someone to kill," I grumbled, standing up and walking into a noxious cloud of Winnie gas that sent me to my knees.

Gasping for air.

"No! No!" I reached up to my desk, desperately seeking something with which to end my suffering. My hand bumped a ceramic mug and I wrapped my hand around it, staring down into the slightly sweetened light roast with cinnamon and cloves ground up and placed in the grounds.

"I thought the spices that made up pumpkin spice were used to ward off evil," I glared at Winnie's butt, but her wagging tail was accompanied by an earth-shaking snore. "Maybe *you* should have been a mercenary. You wouldn't even have to try very hard, you could kill people in your sleep!"

She continued ignoring me.

"Seriously! If the goddess of werewolves knew what your people could do, she'd have made a were-Shepherd race to poison the gods who dare challenge her creation. Wolves are majestic, and you my dear child, are an abomination. Like Stitch and whoever saw mushrooms popping out of the ground and thought 'let me put that in my mouth'."

The dog had no response.

I let out a long sigh, chugging the rest of my coffee and walking it over to the single-serve pod machine. My mug declared that I needed to be "Excused from All Humaning Until Coffee Complete". Another pot would have been a better idea than the single-serve pod, but without a distraction, I might as well just go to sleep.

My eyes went to the large front window by the wooden door again, noticing the bright sun reflecting off the flagpoles and tempered windows all along Main Street. The widget in the bottom corner of my screen announced that this delightful summer day offered nearly three-digit temperatures and thirty percent humidity. Adding to the oppressive feel of the day, there wasn't a soul walking down the street or posted on the outdoor tables and benches.

Coffee in hand, I pressed my face against the window, trying to see the sidewalk in either direction. Heat radiated from the surface and singed my skin, a small sting compared to the crushing agony sitting on my chest.

"Please... someone... please?" I begged the universe, removing my face to drink coffee. I'd left behind a smear of face grease with pore indentations, my finger tracking through the residue in an aimless trance.

My mind wandered back to the time Larry and I had spent a week exchanging messages in the steam of his shower door. It was a never-ending excuse to shower, anticipation building as to whether or not there would be a message when the water hit boiling.

That ended like our relationship, with his mother complaining that it wasn't appropriate.

"Excuse me?"

I screamed and smacked my head against the window, sloshing hot coffee onto my hand and nearly screaming again at the fact that I spilled coffee. My eyes searched the room in a panic, the office door already closed as a woman stood two feet inside of it, her plain jean shorts and shirt unremarkable even as I felt my heart pounding in my chest.

"What? Oh my dog... ow," I tried to stick my whole hand in my mouth to numb the pain.

"Are you..." The woman had dark blonde hair and an average build, her mouth forming several endings to the question she started. "Are..."

"I'm Cynthia, well Cyn, Sharp. Of Sharp Investigations..." I spoke quickly with my hand in my mouth. The words came out as shhhshhh uhh shhh insssss. If we were both snakes or spoke Parseltongue, it would have made perfect sense. As it was, my words reminded me of a balloon losing air and I was fairly certain no one spoke that language.

"I'm sorry, I may be in the wrong place," she searched the office, a look of loss on her face. "Could you point me to someone who..."

I tried to pull my hand out of my mouth. An interesting turn of events from trying to remove my metaphorical foot. Though I rarely tried very hard to remove my foot in social faux pas situations.

People were not my forte.

"Sorry. What are you looking for? Who were you looking for? Do you need me to find someone?" I asked, trying not to alarm her with my desperation. When she shifted uncomfortably, I did my best impersonation of an intelligent and emotionally stable human being. "Did you kill someone? Do you need someone killed? Do you need me to find someone who wronged you so you can arrange for them to be killed?"

The note of hysteria in my voice did not escape my ears and I declared my "normal human being" mask an absolute failure. Winnie's ears lifted when she flopped to the side and let out an annoyed howl at my high-pitched exclamation.

"Oh!" The woman pressed a hand to her chest, and I sensed relief when she spotted Winnie. "I am in the right place. Noah sent me pictures."

My head dropped to my left shoulder and I blinked at her.

"Noah? The man with the ark and the animals?" I asked. Noah was the only religious figure I was into because of the whole animal thing. I cleared my throat when she remained silent, staring at Winnie with a look I would call... wistful. Maybe she was hoping for another flood and thought Winnie was the triggering factor to make that happen.

She was in for a rude awakening if she thought that flood would be made of anything more than tears plucked forcibly from her eyes by Winnie's farts.

"No, my brother. Noah Bergeron?" Her voice went up at the end in question and my memory gave a slight nudge of recognition. "You met while you and your partner were on vacation... or maybe suspension?"

Another ping bounced through my frontal lobe. I couldn't tell if it was the name or the combination of the name with her accent, but I needed more info. I gestured for her to keep going, picking up the woodsy touch of another country in her words.

"Right... You've probably seen the world. My brother lived in Saskatoon, he said he encountered you in the woods while he was working. You were being chased by an angry woman and decided to climb a tree to escape, only the tree you picked was the one he'd been chopping and..."

I held up my hand.

"Please, just stop," I said, my face red and stomach clenched. Somehow the hunt for sasquatch had turned into an attack on Americans after Winnie had eaten a potentially prize-winning pie. Followed by a potentially prize-winning chicken and a definitively prize winning first prize ribbon. The angry mob had sent us scrambling deeper into the woods. I'd needed twelve stitches that day and ended up drunk on top of her brother the next morning, still trying to figure out whether his underwear was as flannel and plaid as his over wear.

He said it would remain as mysterious as the sasquatch I was trying to find because he didn't bone tourists... or he had a bone to pick with tourists... Maybe he'd itched a bone on some tourists?

Either way, we'd left on amicable terms despite my hangover and lady equivalent of blue balls.

"I remember Noah. That's your brother?"

"Yes," she smiled wide. "He told me about the woman looking for Big Foot in the woods from a small town in America. Your depiction of this place made it sound magical and I ended up moving here with my American husband last year. While your stories were told under the influence of far too much bourbon, nothing was exaggerated and I was not disappointed."

Her whole face lit up and I wondered if I would ever look like that talking about my own brother. Then I remembered his children and determined it to be statistically improbable.

"How's he doing? Still Paul Bunyon-ing the woods with his axe and flannel?"

Her face crumbled, hands wringing in front of her. I'd communicated with her brother intermittently, completely unaware that he'd somehow convinced a relative to move to this roadside attraction of questionable repute.

"How did what I said make this place appealing to you? Because I promise, I was pretty clear it was a comic relief sketch in the show of life. I know I was drunk, but I was hiding from my family in Canada for a reason... you know, besides gravy and cheese on French fries. Are you here to beat me up for under-selling the insanity?"

"N- no. He's..." She seemed to fight herself for the right words, my stomach knotting even as my mind coveted the opportunity to do something, anything, besides fall apart.

"He's been taken."

Chapter Five:
Promised Land

I blinked at the woman in front of me and searched her face for signs of humor.

"He... Noah... was... taken?" I asked, more stunned than I had been watching Amber ride Larry. Sex was natural, a grown man who made me feel petite being abducted was not. I was nearly six feet of solid plus-sized snack loving woman and short of stabbing me with a tranquilizer and stuffing me in a potato sack, no one was taking me anywhere without my consent.

They did not make potato sacks big enough to capture someone Noah's size.

"That's the only explanation!" She insisted, giving up all reservations and flopping in my guest chair. "He was due to arrive a few days ago, the payment went through, but he's still not here!"

"I think you might need to start from the beginning and try and make this whole thing sound a little less... Hollywood Tower Hotel," I spoke into my coffee mug, chugging the rest and trying to decide between a refill or something harder. "What day of the week is it?"

"Monday," she answered, despite my question not being directed to anyone. Monday meant I was due at the farm later for animal technician-ing. Monday meant goats, chickens and cows.

Monday meant I needed to stay sober.

Damn, coffee it is.

Oh my dog, I'm upset to have to drink coffee.

I hauled myself out of my desk chair for yet another cup, silently apologizing to the mother bean for my indiscretion. As I selected a flavor, I caught the woman staring at me with distrust.

"It's been a long couple of days, ma'am," I commented, popping another pod in. "But let's get everything down and hope one of us isn't crazy and the other is crazy but competent."

"You think I'm crazy?" She huffed, jumping to her feet and jutting a hip.

"I said let's hope you're not. The only definitively crazy person here is me, but I'm starting not to expect a different result from these investigations, and I do them anyway..." I paused mid-thought. Was I still insane even when I didn't expect a different result? The scientific method is repeating an experiment to confirm its validity... over and over again hoping that it didn't get a different outcome.

I'm not insane, I'm a scientist!

A stupid one, because your experiment does not need repeating.

I had no counterargument for that mental assertion and I blinked at my visitor who appeared to be waiting for a response.

"Did you ask something?"

"I asked if that was supposed to make me feel better?" She huffed and I tried to remember if I was being catty or re-assuring.

No clue.

"I don't know. Do you want my help?" She nodded and I fought between annoyance and relief. It would be nice to have a distraction, but it would be nicer to not have to talk to other humans. "Let's start with some basics, then. What is your name and would you like some coffee?"

"Robin, and no thank you."

I nodded as the machine sputtered and my cup filled.

"Alright Robin, person who doesn't drink coffee and is certain she is not crazy, when did you last speak to Noah?" I put sugar in my coffee and mourned the inky color.

All my oat milk, cream, creamer, and flavor syrups were at Larry's house. Or at least they had been on Friday before he went out of town and my phone met its untimely demise. Who knows what those animals did to my coffee supplies.

Casualties of the cruelty that is love.

"About four days ago. He was on his way to the meeting place with his visa sponsor. I had been coordinating the papers for his arrival, but he doesn't own a cell phone. Once he left his house, the opportunity to communicate was lost until his scheduled arrival yesterday," she wrung her hands in her lap and I watched her over the rim of my coffee cup looking for any indication this was a joke.

Robin was clearly distressed. There were dark circles under her eyes, her socks didn't match each other, and I was fairly certain she hadn't brushed her hair. Not normally an indication of something bad, but her matching nail polish and wrinkle-free clothing indicated she was normally completely in control of all aspects of her existence.

Despite this, her skin radiated a bright energy that baffled my senses. Were there bioluminescent humans or did she hope to detract from her tired appearance with a body shimmer? Would she share where it came from before people started telling me I "looked tired"?

"He could have been delayed," I challenged, watching her eyes darken in annoyance. "His flight could have been canceled or the train derailed. Do you have his travel information? An itinerary of some sort?"

"Ms. Sharp, do you think I'm an idiot?"

I nearly choked on my coffee as I raised a brow in challenge. It was definitely a rhetorical question, but if I answered yes, would it start a fight? My eyes swept over my visitor, assessing her potential.

It wouldn't be a fair fight.

She'd probably gotten way more sleep than me and had a manic glint in her eyes that said never give up, never surrender.

"No?"

Almost as fast as the annoyance crossed her face, it faded back into worry. Resigned, she flopped back into my guest chair. In the process, a half dozen tissues and two tubes of lipstick fell from her pockets.

"My apologies, Ms. Sharp. I'm a bit on edge. His travel was arranged by the immigration assistance agency, but they couldn't give me his travel details as it was a stand-by ticket and there were a few options for departure. Actually, they couldn't even clarify his mode of transportation. When two days had passed from the promised arrival window, I contacted the sponsor again. But the number is disconnected. Every bit of contact information I had is now giving error messages and unavailable notices. Like the company never existed." Her gaze had drifted to the front office window, hands clutching each other with white knuckles and some of her nervous energy transferred to me. "The main woman I spoke with, Ruth, said she was mobility challenged. But I can't find any record of a Ruth and no one in the area knows of a wealthy mobility challenged woman."

"Are you sure the person you worked with was a woman? Did you get the impression she was mobility challenged? Can you verify that she's 'older'? Or are these all self-provided descriptions by the bamboozler?" I asked, not wanting to waste too much time on the mysterious Ruth.

"I'm fairly confident in the female part, as I heard her voice. I also unintentionally overheard a shouted exclamation by a man about needing more lube on her dildo. The older part came from her word choice. Just an old-world style of speech... the mobility challenged was just something I took her word for... do you think it was a lie? Would that impact sexual ability?"

"Not in my experience." I shuddered at the mention of older people and dildos... it meant I'd benefit from asking my mom about her sex life.

No child should benefit from asking about their parent's sex life.

Sure, I existed because of it, but that doesn't mean I needed to *know* about it.

"Alright, let's..." I rubbed my face and put my mind to work. "Alright, let's start with some... background? Maybe... I don't know. Usually family visits on a tourist visa, and your husband can be the... visiting party person with citizenship..."

A dull ache throbbed in my frontal lobe and I tried to remember how people came to this country. Tourist visas worked for some time... he may not have been eligible for a social security number on a tourist visa if he intended to work but he could apply for one maybe... or steal one. I literally just looked up citizenship in the last few months and somehow retained nothing.

Well, nothing except the certainty immigration was unnecessarily difficult, expensive and not for the easily distracted. Since I was poor, easily distracted and lazy, I'd relied heavily on Carla to clear up Lizandro's paperwork and in exchange I promised Winnie's bomb sniffing services to some sort of diplomat or maybe politician?

Not sure what she could offer in terms of finding immigrants who didn't arrive at their destination.

"Noah had... an incident a few years back. He's not eligible for a tourist visa. He may not be eligible for a sponsored visa, but the woman, Ruth supposedly, said she'd take care of it." Sucking her bottom lip into her mouth, she started worrying it with her teeth. "It didn't seem right. I mean, he ended up on a watch list because of a minor incident in a bar-"

"Time out, watch list?" I stared at her with my full attention. It felt similar to finding a cookie in my pocket when I thought I'd run out of snacks. "How was Noah on a watchlist? He said he didn't drink... or maybe he didn't drink with women? Sports women? Women dressed for sports..."

She offered a sheepish smile.

"He was in the bar, but he wasn't drunk. Hockey was on, he enjoyed watching hockey with other people, and the bar catered to a crowd that was pretty easy-going about their team loyalty. The ref made what Noah considered a bad call. Normally, he would have been met with aggressive ribbing and physical disagreement. Only he was rooting for the Canadians and it was not really the best time to be watching sports in America and cheering for the Maple Leaves." A ghost of laughter touched her eyes before fading out again. "It was the Winter Olympics and he made a comment that was overheard by... What are they called? The people who steal your freedom in exchange for security?"

"Homeland Security?" I offered, though that was just the tip of the freedom thieving iceberg. "T.S.A. or the Marshalls? Texas Rangers? Republican justices if you're a woman? S.H.I.E.L.D. sometimes but only under the control of Hydra."

"I'm fairly certain it's the first one," her gaze drifted away, eyes unfocused. "The woman said that a sponsored visa was a monetary guarantee of appropriate social behavior. That for a small fee, she would put up the required money to bring him here."

"You paid a stranger to monetarily secure your brother's compliance in this country?" I asked, perplexed that if money could get such compliance from immigrants, how come the country didn't use this power to stop sexual assault and people who steal your coffee from the pick-up counter.

"That sounds strange in your wording, but yes. Like she was paying for the right to monitor him and I was paying for a babysitter..." Her eyes sharpened at me again and I froze. "That's not even a thing is it?"

Her eyes continued to impale me in place as I stared at my coffee.

"Uhh... not my area of knowledge, but money opens a lot of doors here. How much did she put up to guarantee his behavior while he was here? You pay the fee, she puts up the bond, more or less... How does she get that money back?" I drank a big swallow of coffee as I contemplated googling immigration, but past experience had taught me there was no comprehensive "for dummies" article on the topic.

I assume it was to keep immigration lawyers in business, though I imagine many of them fell into the "dummies" category.

"About half a million," she shrugged, and I had to scrape my jaw off the floor. "What? She said she had a lot of money and she thought she would use it to help others. Growing it with small fees instead of the banks earning off her hard work. As for the return process, when I asked what conditions had to be met... she told me not to worry about it."

"She told you not to worry about half a million dollars? How are you not supposed to worry about that?" I gaped at her and she shifted uncomfortably.

"I mean... it's not my money. Ruth said she could afford it and I missed my brother. I just wanted him here... for the birth..."

She rubbed her abdomen and I felt like someone had pulled back the curtain on The Wizard.

Never would I have knowingly been in a room with a pregnant woman this long. I had fears about contagion and insanity cases that were quite popular in fiction and 90's true crime.

"Great... just great..." I muttered, waking up my partner who scented the air cautiously. Winnie approached the woman with great caution, probably noticing for the first time she sounded like two living things undergoing cellular respiration. Ears flat, she crawled forward on her belly and gave a cautious sniff of the woman's abdomen.

One sniff.

Two sniff.

She let out a yelp and ran. Winnie left the room, scrambled upstairs to my apartment where I heard her claws clatter on the hardwood floor and the thunk of her leaping onto the bed and sending it sliding a few inches.

Lucky dog, I thought as I looked longingly at all of the exits.

Robin cleared her throat and my eyes drifted back to her. Despite her condition and the imminent threat to humanity it represents, she didn't seem like a bad person. Normal people did terrifying things under the influence of pregnancy hormones and compared to stories I've heard, wanting her brother here enough to willfully break the law didn't seem that bad.

Until he disappeared.

The landline in my office rang and I picked up the receiver, still pondering all that I had learned.

"Sharp Investigations."

"I've been calling your cell for an hour! Where the hell are you, Cyn?"

I stared at the handset and blinked.

"This is a landline. So I'm in my office?" I checked my watch and I still had an hour before work. "Who is this?"

I stared at the handset, trying to get the caller to stick their head out and say *hello*. It was a black push button phone with an internal bell and hammers I'd unearthed at a yard sale. What it lacked in fancy features like wireless function and caller ID, it made up for in being heavy enough to use as a weapon and continuing to work in a power outage.

Features you cannot ask the man at Best Buy for without getting followed around the store.

"Are you listening to me? It's Carla you dunce. We were supposed to meet the diplomat to go over security for the event Friday night! I've been getting stink eye for half an hour from his assistant waiting for you! Now Conri has to go and I have to sit here with this guy!" She was practically exploding with frustration and I couldn't hold back.

I snickered, loudly and with complete disregard for her public servant predicament.

"Stop laughing, Cynthia!"

"You are a trained former government agent with skills that rival Liam Neeson but hotter. What the hell do you have to fear from a tubby politician with more money and ego than common sense?" It came out garbled with laughter as my body doubled over in a pitch that bordered on hysteria.

"Shut up, Cyn!" She hissed and her voice quieted as she spoke softly and soothingly to a man with a voice like gravel in a cement truck. Without any real knowledge of the diplomat I was serving, it was hard to conjure a face to go with the voice, but the word 'hot' came to mind. "Get a new cell phone and get your ass over here after you finish your work day at the dairy! Conri is leaving, so you'll have to meet him the day of and make sure his limbs don't depart his body in a fiery explosion!"

She hung up and I glanced at the receiver, considering a moment that I should have hung up first for the satisfaction of slamming it down. It was probably the last opportunity I'd have to use a landline with someone yelling at me for at least the next forty-eight hours.

Missed opportunities, I lamented internally. My eyes looked for Winnie, hoping she'd convince someone new to call me. Instead, they landed on a pregnant Canadian with mis-matched socks. The dog in question was cowering in bed where I wanted to be.

"Right... I need to buy a new cell phone. Do you have emails and call logs from when you spoke to the immigration agency?" I asked her, not bothering to soothe her fears regarding my conversation with a "former government agent" that seemed to have made her go pale and clammy.

"Yes. Ms. Sharp, are you going to tell," her voice dropped to a whisper. "The authorities about what I did?"

"That you had sex and made a new life form from two previously genetically inadequate pieces of biological material?" I whispered back and her cheeks tinged pink.

"No! About trying to circumvent the law to bring my brother here?"

I shrugged as I started to gather my things to head to the mobile phone store.

"It doesn't really seem necessary. Excessive pride in one's country of origin is a disease more than a crime and I don't punish the ill. Send the documents to this email," I scribbled my email address on a notepad and ripped off the top sheet. "Any voicemails or communications, anything related to this, send it to me."

"So you'll find Noah?" Tears shimmered in her eyes and I held up a finger.

"I'll try but only if you stop crying immediately or leave and do it outside."

She barreled toward me and gripped my torso in a death hug that was designed to maim. I could feel the tears still dripping down her face and soaking into my shirt.

"Thank you! Thank you!"

Already failing to follow instructions, this does not bode well, I thought as I patted her back awkwardly and she blew her nose on my sleeve.

Chapter Six: Pick Up Sticks

"For the last time-"

"For the last time," parroted the little boy as he moved his hands in a talking gesture. With every mimic he swayed more of his hips and made the collection of children laugh louder. ,

"I'm serious, I will throw-"

"I'm serious, I will throw-" He was now using an even higher pitched voice, his mocking teapot pose an insult to my beloved Mrs. Potts. His hip wiggle, an insult to women everywhere.

If our hips wiggled, it was probably because we were off balance after years of being forced to carry a purse when they wouldn't let us have clothes with pockets.

"That's it." I let out a loud sharp whistle.

"That's it," he mocked and blew a raspberry, sending his audience of his peers into a fit of laughter until the tell-tale jingle and thundering of paws descended on the area. Several of the little demons gasped while two started shoving their way to the back of the crowd.

My parrot had yet to turn around.

Sgt. Winnie arrived beside me, tongue lolling out of the side of her mouth. She had clearly been running amuck or napping after running amuck and looked like she smelled delightful. As predicted, her paws were coated in a slimy brown substance that was either manure or mud and it coated all four legs and the underside of her torso.

She looked absolutely perfect for the mission at hand.

"Winnie," I gestured at the back of the boy and she raised a brow. When I hitched a thumb, she leapt toward his back, right as he decided to turn around. He let out a startled yelp, taking two paws to the chest and crashing to the ground with my dog on top of him. Winnie started licking his face as he screamed and burst into tears.

"Winnie, off."

She pranced toward me and I handed her a treat from my pocket. The little boy had landed in grass and despite his completely injury free descent, he wouldn't stop crying. After a ruffle of Winnie's ears, she trotted back toward the barn, tail in the air and teeth munching her treat.

"Oh my dog, get over it. As I was saying," my focus remained on the group while some Karen's crotch fruit picked himself up off the ground. On a good day, I found children terrifying. I hadn't had a good day since Saturday night so children were like mosquitos, sucking the life out of me until I took initiative and swatted one down. "Everything with dairy comes from a female animal lactating. Lactation is the biological female response to birth that sends a signal to release the milk from the designated location."

I'd learned long ago not to use words like "mammary gland" and "reproductive organs".

"So... those dangling things are... cow boobs?" A girl with a braided high ponytail asked and I nodded. "Eww!! Boobs are gross! My brother tapes pictures of them to his bedroom wall!"

The rest of the group joined in and I wanted to rub the tension from my temples. I lifted my hands and studied them. They were still coated in questionable gunk that I swore not to smear on my face.

Again.

Though I'd managed to make it two days without having a complete post-relationship breakdown, everything was dulled into a muted grey haze. Even putting the kid in his place with an overly friendly dog didn't bring the same joy it normally would have. The satisfaction was fleeting at best, and at worst I felt guilty for giving in to my childish whims.

Aside from re-uniting a missing Canadian with his pregnant sister, I didn't really have anything to look forward to.

After reviewing all of the information Robin sent me and calling in a few favors, I was still struggling to determine who or what would want a Canadian lumberjack. The IP address for all of the communications came back to the public library, but there was evidence that the IP address had been cloned and no one in my circle had the tech savvy to hack it.

Mrs. Margot, one of the town elders, had a niece who worked or acted as a hacker. While it was unclear if that was her job, hobby or life's mission, I researched the subject heavily. Most of it made absolutely zero sense, but I'm fairly certain she's a grey hat. Some sort of chaotic neutral who does what she wants and helps people if she feels like it but would be equally fine watching the world burn. She protected her family and the people she loved, but she had no problem protecting them by sending the would-be aggressor up the river to a bigger fish with a grudge that would eliminate the threat.

Essentially, she was my tech savvy clone and I wondered why we weren't BFFs.

Probably because my internet usage was limited to ordering snacks and coffee in bulk.

I'd asked Mrs. Margot for help but apparently her niece the "cracker" had "gone dark" and would "return to the web" soon. I tried to find another grey hat or maybe a white hat, but I just ended up on a website called Lids and ordered a few new ball caps.

Overall, none of it had seemed unusual except the fact that Mrs. Glen Margot refused to refer to her niece as a hacker and insisted it was a mispronunciation of the word cracker. It was proven by the fact her niece hadn't washed a dish in her entire life and didn't own a vacuum.

If Mrs. Margot hadn't been one thousand years old when I was born, I'd have tried to make my case that she was in fact a hacker and *also* a lazy housekeeper. But as she was old, stubborn, and the legal owner of my business office and residence, I elected to let it go for a roof over my head and a place to sit between work shifts. Unfortunately, it meant I was no closer to the online identity of the so-called immigration assistance organization.

It also meant I needed to work on my poker face when I was around her because hearing an old white lady call her family member a cracker was hilarious.

None of the airlines had records of passengers with the name Noah Bergeron, and the bus companies and trains didn't require names. It would have been a genius way to smuggle illegal goods into the country if those goods weren't a person who was, for all intents and purposes, missing.

Also there were no illegal goods I wanted to smuggle from Canada because ice wine was allowed across the border freely and no one made you declare it.

Aside from declaring it was time to drink ice wine.

"Do all female animals make milk?" A little boy shouted, his hand waving in the air. At his height, he was probably used to being overlooked, but I was tall enough that anything short of a maze of skyscrapers gave me a bird's eye advantage. He reminded me of a young Larry with his glasses and too-thin frame, a fact that poked a hole in my fractured heart.

"Yes. But only once the female animal has given birth. Pregnancy and female chromosomes are not enough to begin the biological process of lactose production," I answered.

"So, can you make us some milk for our afternoon cookies? Or are you just fat?" My parrot snickered and the whole class joined in.

I was officially done with children.

"Whatever. Who wants to see the collection tanks?" No one responded and I shrugged. "Great. Go over there and do whatever you want. Try sneaking up behind the donkey. She likes that."

I gestured toward the goat enclosure and walked away without a second glance. The goats sat beside the horses, donkeys and our one alpaca that showed up in the middle of the night and required all farm hands to sign an NDA over how it came into our possession.

They'd probably be safe running around the farm half supervised.

That or they would die, an excellent demonstration of natural selection for those who survived.

Either way, the school signed a release of liability waiver. One that their parents agreed with in the field trip permission slip and the farm required for any and all student visits.

A measure that was added after my "incident" at the Dayton zoo.

If anyone was going to end up coated in giraffe afterbirth after running away from a rampaging ostrich, it was me. An ostrich who was chasing me because I tripped when Amber tried to shove me into a trash can and I fell into the path of the angry running bird. The benefit to being tall was I escaped the bird, but ended up in the personnel only area where a giraffe was being born. A picture of the class with the newborn giraffe still graced the walls of the local K-12 and every midnight black pajama attempt I'd made to remove it was foiled.

The day ended with Larry being the only kid who would sit next to me and two hours of "Larry and Cyn, sitting in a tree". Amber got a stern warning, I got coated in giraffe goo, Larry refused to acknowledge my existence for a month and the school got a lawyer.

Like always, the only one who'd suffered any consequences was me.

"What are you doing, Cynthia?" Joseph shouted at me as I wandered into the barn and plucked a thermometer from a deep sink. He was the manager of the dairy, but I recently learned he was also the owner paying a cute little old couple to pose as the owners for marketing purposes. Despite being from the city, he adopted the country chic of plaid flannel shirts and jeans with cowboy boots. All of which were crisp, clean and had no business being on a working ranch.

They were, however, much more appealing to look at than the green Peter Pan tights I'd seen him in once.

"Working, Joseph," I brushed past the short, round man and proceeded to the collection tank. His flannel was two sizes too small and the buttons looked like the cartoon eyes of Roger Rabbit when he was in danger.

Despite my clear dismissal, he waddled behind me and kept talking.

"You're supposed to be leading a field trip group. Where are the kids?" He demanded, breath catching as he fought to get air and yell at me simultaneously.

"They're playing with the goats," I answered, crouching down beside the stainless-steel container and donning rubber gloves to open the little door on the lid. Inserting the thermometer, I compared the reading to the digital display and marked the value of both in a spreadsheet. I repeated the process at the other three drums nearby after sterilizing the thermometer between each.

I thought Joseph had decided to walk away until the soft wheeze behind me offered warning that he intended to continue this conversation. My nearly leveled out heart rate spiked again.

"Why are they playing with goats, Cynthia?" He demanded, and I slammed the last cylinder door shut to glare at him. "What happens if one of them gets hurt?"

"Because they didn't want to listen to me, and I didn't want to murder them. So, I sent them off on their own. You know better than to put me in charge of class trips, Joseph," I shouted, slamming the lid open on the trashcan and tossing the gloves inside. "It's included in the waiver, if one of them gets hurt, we call a medical professional."

"They could be seriously injured! What happens if one of them dies?" He paled and his voice cracked.

"Then we call a damn undertaker, Joseph! Flip through your 1980s rolodex and figure it out! You and I both know that children terrify me! I have zero control over them or my reactions to their crap and yet you keep making the awful decision to have me lead the groups. Today, I led the group to knowledge and when I couldn't make them learn, they were let loose to either live or die on their own."

"This isn't some damn metaphor about leading horses to water. These are children who are visiting and someone has to be in charge!" He shouted back, but without any real conviction. It was unclear if he knew he was wrong or he had heard about my break-up with Larry and decided not to test my self-control. The man was maintaining a pretty decent space buffer between us and I snarled at him in anger. "We're technically responsible if they get hurt."

"Then you do it! Stop day drinking and pretending to know anything about what the farm hands are doing and escort children around. Take them to the ice cream shop and get them hopped up on sugar. Let them meet the fake owners and take pictures. Explain about reproductive organs, get mocked, mimicked and asked if you're pregnant, and then we will talk about whether you pay me enough to ever do it again!" I advanced and he retreated, holding up his hands in surrender.

"Let's just calm down," he tried in his spooked horse voice and I launched myself forward only to feel an arm wrap around my waist and pull me back. I slammed into something hard that smelled of citrus and pine, Joseph scurrying away before I could launch another attack.

"Yeah! You better run!" I shouted after him, struggling against the arms wrapped around me.

"Chica," the warm smooth Cuban voice spoke softly into my ear and I felt all the fight drain out of me. In its place was a heat and a tingling that reminded me his voice alone was foreplay. It was why I'd been ignoring his emails and text messages for months... all two of them. "We need to talk."

My body turned and I found my face inches away from Sgt. Ian Cruz.

Chapter Seven:
Reasonable Threat

F our years ago, I'd completed Basic Training and fought for a spot in the canine program of military police school. No one could deny that while I was not an obedient soldier, nor a particularly competent one, I was determined and deadly. Two factors that convinced my fellow recruits to stand aside and let me have the slot for MP canine training.

No one thought I'd make it through the program, but they let me go anyway.

Winnie, Sgt. Winnifred Pupperson, was named by a breeder's daughter after her favorite movie villain. Winnie was the most disciplined pupil in her litter. She arrived at Lackland four months before I did with more commendations and recommendations than any dog previously brought in by an outside breeder.

At which point, she washed out more potential handlers than any other dog in the Army.

On paper, we were both labeled stubborn, impulsive, food-motivated and brave. The last only ever admitted grudgingly and under extreme duress.

Sgt. Ian Cruz was the training sergeant over my class, and he had witnessed her break the will of at least two of the previous handlers. Whether he thought we could succeed together or was encouraged to get rid of both of us, the pairing was an unprecedented success that not even the Director of the Army would willingly take credit for.

A success that foiled an arms heist, blew up a marketplace, thwarted a terror threat and caused an international incident at a beer and wiener festival in Germany. For every success we had together in the Army, we were equally skilled at demolishing things people were still actively using.

Like the state of Florida.

For some reason people were still using it... and I'd failed to demolish it.

A double insult.

Through it all though, Ian Cruz had never managed to completely disappear on me. He, Winnie, a couple of deployment buddies, and a few scars were the only parts of my Army career I couldn't quite shake.

"I'm not really in a talking mood," I told his liquid chocolate eyes and I fought the urge to lick his neck and see if he tasted as good as he smelled. His smooth skin had a smattering of stubble along his jaw and his hair brushed his ears, plain black T-shirt and jeans made him look casually sexy and un-groomed by military standards.

The sharp movements of his eyes reminded me that he worked for Army Criminal Intelligence and he didn't do anything without an order from the top. The CIC had sent him into more than one mess in this area, and every time he got what he wanted, he walked away.

He was a great help so long as you didn't expect him to share anything... or stay.

"What are you in the mood for, chica?" He asked in a husky voice that sent my heart rate into overdrive.

"Violence," I murmured against his chest before bringing my knee up into his gut and stomping down on his foot. The maneuver was completed with a drop-knee sweep kick that sent him ass first onto the dirt floor of the barn.

Sweeping my way back to standing, I stood over him braced for revenge.

The bastard started laughing.

"Feeling better, chica?" He smirked from the ground and I attempted to stomp on his fingers. When that failed, I whistled for Winnie and she ran out of a barn stall, scented the air and zeroed in on her target. "Oh, come on!"

His plea was drowned by the jingling of her dog tags. With a hearty grunt, he was flat on the ground under my canine, having his face cleaned with her tongue. Winnie's tail went full helicopter, spinning around as she leapt off and pounced toward him from new angles. Each new attack was coupled with a snuffle, and I was disappointed to learn my dog would not actually bite him.

Not surprised, she was not a violent dog.

Just disappointed.

I really wanted to bite him and I was hoping she would take care of that for me.

"Can I get some help, chica?" He asked between Winnie kisses.

"Fine. Winnie, place," I ordered, and she pranced back to flop onto the ground beside me. "But that's the last time I'm helping you."

"Unfortunate..." He spoke rolling gracefully back to standing and looking completely undisturbed by my attack. "Because I need your help."

Joseph sent me home with pay and I found myself sitting in Suzie's Diner across from Ian Cruz and considering the most promising options for eating my feelings. While French fries and a milkshake were a given, I couldn't decide if I wanted a bacon cheeseburger or a cheeseburger with a plate of bacon on the side.

In a tribute to Ron Swanson, I considered just ordering all of the bacon in the restaurant and putting it on everything.

Winnie would probably pee in my shoes if she found out I didn't share and I didn't want to wait for that much bacon to cook.

"Remember the last time we were here?" He asked, glancing at the menu and out the window. His body language was relaxed, but there was a steady tension in the rippling muscles beneath his tightly fitted shirt.

He was on high alert and playing tourist.

"When I got abducted at gunpoint and marched to Mo's where I shot off a man's hand? No. Why do you ask?" I scoffed, downing the iced coffee that was delivered to my table by default by the owner, Suzanne Quentin Williams.

Her parents must have thought they were clever naming her Suzie-Q, though her age indicated maybe she is *the* Suzie-Q. Either way, the diner was vintage and timeless. As was the owner's shift dresses, high pony and constantly changing hair color.

"Cyn, are you OK?" I looked at Ian and raised a brow at him.

"Why do you care?" I asked, gulping more coffee and popping French fries in my mouth after they mysteriously appeared. "Whatever the reason you're here, you'll leave as soon as it's over. No reason to get too close. I was fine before you showed up and I'll be fine after you leave... just like always. So let's get down to why you're here."

"I always care, Cyn. There's only so much I can do... for now," his voice held an edge that reminded me of when I'd spent the night in his arms. "I hate leaving you."

His words brought back more of the parts I could remember. We'd gone to bed when I was totally wasted and I woke up half-dressed hungry and hungover. The physical condition came with the realization that I couldn't sleep with Cruz, not without hurting Larry. So, I turned down Sgt. Sexy and entered a committed relationship with Larry. Larry and I had openly confessed our love and it was all white picket fences.

At least that's what I thought.

Being that I was an idiot, the joke was on me.

Ha freaking ha, I scowled at the thought and Cruz gave me a sympathetic look that I wanted to punch off his handsome face.

"Don't look at me like that. I don't need your pity, concern or care. I just need bacon, cheese and this conversation to end quickly," I snapped, and he offered me another smirk.

"Why? Do you have somewhere to be? Your boss asked you not to come back the rest of the week."

"It's Thursday! One day does not make a permanent vacation," I paused when a plate stacked six high of four bacon strip planks appeared in front of me with a stack of cheese slices. "Thank you."

The waitress gave me a sympathetic smile and rubbed circles on my back before walking away.

"Damn small towns," I grumbled into my bacon and cheese. If she hadn't come bearing everything I wanted in life, I'd have been pissed. As it was, I had bacon and cheese.

Who needs men with bacon and cheese?

"Do you speak out loud and things just magically appear?"

"I don't know. Should we test it? I want you to burst into flames." My eyes watched him for signs of spontaneous combustion.

Nothing.

"Maybe it only works with food. Try conjuring me some hot sauce?" He laughed at his own joke.

"No way. Order it from the wait staff like the rest of the world. Can we just get on with this? What's so important you needed

to crawl out from under your special ops rock to hassle me?"
I folded up a slice of cheese and wrapped bacon around it.
When the cheese was completely covered, I stuck it in my
mouth and let out a soft moan.

Cruz adjusted his position across the table from me.

"Damn, chica," he whispered, his husky voice liquid fire.
"What else makes you moan when you put it in your mouth?"

I kicked him in the shin under the table and he laughed.

"I missed you. All your love taps and affectionate touch-
es," he smiled, fingers inching toward my cheese and bacon.
I pulled them out of his reach and started wrapping both
around my French fries. A container of ranch dressing appeared and I offered a muffled thanks to the passing wait staff
around cheesy bacon fries.

Cruz inched his finger closer, I began fondling my knife
and trying to decide where to stab him that would cause the
most pain but the least amount of mess due to blood loss.
In my experience, hands were incredibly sensitive but they
didn't bleed long if you stabbed them in just the right spot.
Sensing Ian might be in danger, Suzie appeared with an order
pad to stop him from stealing my food.

"What can I get ya?" She asked, but his eyes stayed fixed on
me as I licked ranch off my fingers, knife forgotten when she
placed a container of guacamole beside my fries.

"I'll just share what she's having," his voice dropped another octave and Suzie's eyes moved between us. When I
reached for my knife, Suzie pulled it off the table and gave me
a stern look.

"Bad, Cynthia. No knives. And you? Ruin that body eating the way she does? You can have a grilled chicken salad and an iced tea," her gaze lingered a little too long on his perfectly sculpted biceps trying to escape his shirt. "But I'll let you have a side of fries."

Tucking her pen and notepad away, she gave me a reassuring pat on the back.

"Haha! You have to eat salad," I mocked around a mouthful of cheese and potatoes.

"Why is everyone treating you like you're fragile?" His brows were furrowed and I looked away.

The last person I wanted to tell that I'd been traded in for a smaller model was the formidably sexy Sgt. Ian Cruz. Sure, he'd met Amber and found her terrifying, but Larry had once claimed the same and look how that ended.

"Don't worry about it. What case are you here for?" I asked, smiling when a cheeseburger with onion rings and BBQ sauce was dropped off in front of me. His salad arrived moments later. "Is it about the missing Canadian?"

"What missing Canadian?" His eyes never left my lips, even after I wiped the ranch off.

"There was a woman in my office Monday. She tried to smuggle her brother into the country, but the day he was due to arrive, nothing. Once a few days had passed, she discovered the company she worked with had completely disappeared," his face went blank, the perfect secret-keeping Stepford soldier.

"How old is he?" Ian's voice had gone emotionless as well.

"Uhhh.... Thirty something I think. I don't remember his age in the folder, but he was definitely mid-twenties at least when I met him a few years back."

"So this isn't a case of child trafficking. You met him?" His cocked eyebrow spoke volumes, but I elected to ignore them while he took in his sad salad and the small plate of fries dropped off by a goth kid in all black with hot pink hair streaks.

"Yeah, in Canada. It was sort of an accident. His sister came to this area because of a conversation I had with him. She married an American, and now she's pregnant and wants her brother here with her." I wrapped my mouth around the massive burger and took a bite that dinosaurs would be proud of. "I'm guessing by your face you're here for something else. What's your gig?"

"The diplomat's party tomorrow night," he said, taking a tiny bite of lettuce dipped into dressing that was likely fat free. "I heard you're attending?"

"Attending is a bit strong. Winnie is working the gate to repay a favor and sweeping the house before guests arrive." A coffee refill appeared and I gulped it. "Nothing major. In the interest of not burning any bridges, or diplomats, we've been brushing up on her explosives detection skills this past month. She's still flawless and undignified."

"Who do you owe a favor to?"

"Carla," I shrugged. "She helped me with a paperwork issue and in exchange for correcting a clerical error, she promised Winnie's services. Said it was just an estate and a paranoid diplomat. What's so special about this dude that he warrants CIC protection?"

Cruz took several bites of his salad and I almost let out an exasperated sigh. He was measuring his words, picking and choosing what he deemed necessary for me to know. It was the most frustrating part about working with him and an even greater reminder as to why I couldn't trust him.

Not completely.

"Remember a few months ago when I was here to keep Carla's identity a secret and take down a corrupt politician?" I nodded. "The man who sold the spy equipment, Andrew Scott, had been of interest for some time. In his work as a foreign correspondent, he made some enemies on both sides. One of them was Conri Kade, son of a madman trying to destroy small villages in Africa. Conri turned in his father in exchange for asylum, but Andrew Scott sold him out for a big fat payday. Now he is paranoid, scared and heavily guarded."

"Why have a party at all then?" I asked, swiping the last of my fries through the last of my guacamole.

"It's not really a party. It's a fundraising benefit to rebuild more of the places his father destroyed. He's been hosting them for years, without actually attending, but there's a big fish on the line who won't pay out unless Conri attends and the money that could be donated would rebuild the village and add some much needed infrastructure," his words sent my neck hair standing on end.

"Sounds like a trap."

"Which is why you, Winnie and I are going to keep him alive," he picked up the check and looked down at the number. "How come the only thing on here is my salad and a little note that says, 'Chin up, tiger'?"

I tugged the paper from his hand and offered Suzie my best death glare.

"Because if I look down, I'll trip and she's tired of cleaning my blood from the front of her business," I offered. It was technically not a lie. Just last week I tripped over a leaf because I thought it was a hole in the sidewalk and tried to avoid it. I threw a twenty on top of the ticket and climbed out of the seat, turning to leave.

"I can buy my own lettuce, chica," Cruz started to pull out his wallet but I was already moving, and then I was flat on the floor crawling away when the bell over the door rang.

Larry just walked into Suzie's Diner with Amber.

Chapter Eight: Back in Black

"Are you sure you can handle this?" Carla asked me for the one hundred and thirty third time. Counting my mom, Seth, Mo and random townspeople, the count of times I was asked this exact question was well into the five-digit range.

"Yes. For the love of dog, yes. But if all of you don't stop asking me, I'm going on a cheese eating rampage which I will let Winnie join and then trap the gas in a dome encompassing the whole town until your vocal cords burn out and you can never ask anyone anything again, ever."

It was too many words for a single breath and I was panting with spit at the corner of my mouth.

Her small smile said we both knew it was an idle threat.

Looking down at myself, I was mildly impressed at how professional I appeared. The fitted black suit over white button down gave me an FBI look. I'd slicked my hair into a low bun and found a wireless earpiece for my phone so I could have hands-free communication throughout the night.

Even in my dress greens I hadn't looked this competent.

Competent or stylish. Perhaps the Bureau was on to something with this black suit, white shirt look. If I had a pair of aviators, I'd be Seeley Booth without the belt buckles.

"But he was out at the diner, with *her*," Carla narrowed her eyes and I resisted the urge to ask if she'd like a litter box for all her catty drama. I was grateful for the support, but once I started down the path of angry fuel-filled ranting, I wasn't stopping until I ripped them both apart with words so sharp... "Everyone said they ate together and she was holding his hand!"

Happy thoughts. Happy Thoughts.

"I was out with Cruz. We broke up. He can do whatever he wants with whoever he wants and I don't care. I've lost the privilege of calling him an idiot to his face, now I just judge silently from afar." I shrugged even as the tight band of anxiety around my chest squeezed. Seeing him with her had hurt. Acting like it didn't bother me when he let her take his hand as they walked in hurt even more. Before he could see me, I'd dropped to the ground, crawled behind the bar counter, and ran out the back door into the alley, fighting off panic and the urge to hyperventilate.

When it came to fight or flight in the face of an ex-boyfriend, I would always choose flight.

Especially when fighting had more or less been foreplay before it all came crashing down.

Ian had seen the whole thing and said nothing, making him my new favorite person in this town. Even temporarily, the reprieve from having to address my anger, hurt, and jealousy was well worth the horrifying stains on my knees. Instead of forcing me to talk, Ian took me to the grocery store, bought me bags of candy, two quarts of ice cream and walked me home. He dimmed the lights, brewed a pot of coffee and left without ever once uttering a meaningless platitude.

If he wasn't so prone to secrets and deception, I'd have fallen in love with him for that act alone.

"Everyone knows you and Ian are just business. What the hell was he doing there with her?" She slammed down an ID card and a matte black semi-automatic handgun. She'd managed not to get either in the melted puddles of ice cream I hadn't cleaned up since I had it for breakfast... and lunch... also an evening snack. It would have been dinner if Carla hadn't shown up with a microwave meal full of actual nutritional value. The woman insisted that if I didn't eat a vegetable, I'd pass out, the diplomat would be murdered and it would be exclusively my fault.

Her parenting skills of wielding guilt as a weapon were really coming along.

"It doesn't matter. None of it matters. What do I need that for?"

I gestured to the gun and ID on the counter. After one last concerned look, she switched to business mode.

"It was requested that you be armed. Once you sweep the perimeter of the house, you'll be posted at the gate until the last guest arrives. They'd like you to maintain the perimeter throughout the evening. Ian will be inside with me and several others, keeping eyes on Conri Kade, in various levels of camouflage. The interior has been cleared and all staff have been vetted. The only unknowns are the guests and their escorts. Have you had a chance to review the names and faces in the book?"

I nodded, flicking through names and faces I'd memorized in my mind. Conri's father's accomplices spanned the globe, with members of all nationalities present. Remembering the second binder of known allies and security, I wondered again how certain Conri was of his men.

His father's men could be anyone.

I looked at the handgun she'd set on the counter before walking to my nightstand and pulling out a shoulder holster. Slipping off the suit jacket, I attached the hardware and pulled out Winnie's armor.

"Does she need that?" Carla asked, watching me clip it into place.

"Am I the only human who will be armed?" I asked, not pausing in my work.

"No. Everyone on gate detail will be armed," Carla confirmed and I nodded.

"Then yes, she needs it. The only person I trust to be armed around her safely is me," I double checked the Kevlar and added her name to the side in Velcro. It still said Sgt. Winnifred Pupperson, but if I was qualified to work supporting a government operation, she was qualified to outrank me again.

"Are you ready then?" She asked and I glanced once more around my tiny apartment.

"I memorized the faces in the binder, have dog, have gun, I am wearing pants... I guess so. Want me to follow you in the Jeep?" I asked, but she shook her head. Leading me down the stairs and out the fire door to the alley that ran behind my building.

"Conri wants a very specific visual for tonight. We'll be driving in that," she pointed to a sleek black SUV with glossy paint and small flags affixed to the quarter panel behind the front wheel well.

"Spiffy. It's getting covered in dog hair," I declared, popping open the back door for Winnie to leap in. "I wish the sun would go down already."

I blinked up at the not yet setting sun, still baffled by daylight at eight in the evening.

We were way too far from the equator.

But most places closer to the equator were also closer to Florida... and... well... Florida.

"Are you sure you're up for-"

"Ask me again and I'll throw you in that dumpster," I warned her, rounding the car and taking up the passenger seat while Carla slid into the driver's side.

"OK, but you know if you ever need to talk..." She turned the engine over and music filled the car. It was beat driven and featured a trance quality string instrument that belonged in a Bollywood movie. The undercurrent of a shimmering tambourine added a majestic quality to a sultry melody.

"Yeah, I know," I said, resting my head on the window and letting the song carry me away.

We'd barely been driving an hour when I no longer recognized the surroundings.

Instead of farms mixed with family homes and the estates of the wealthy, we were in a no man's land of trees and the twilight of the setting sun. I could see shadows in the distance and hear the rumble of cars, but on a normal night I imagined it would be impossible to hear anything beyond the whisper of leaves.

"Where are we?" I asked softly, not wanting to break the trance created by music and twilight.

"This is where the government puts people they don't want to be found who could also benefit from not being found. You met his assistant at Conri's actual living quarters, but this secluded spot is for events and parties hosted by people considered dead or excommunicated by their own people. Technically, this place doesn't exist."

"Cool," I said to myself and Winnie nudged the side of my neck in agreement.

We'd always wanted to be "mysteriously disappeared".

Carla turned onto a road lined with solar powered stake lights and a looming mansion came into view. The entire forest shifted to make room for a house more grandiose than all of old school Hollywood. Pavement gave way to brick and expanded into a wide circle before a sweeping staircase.

The Carter household, Amber's family, had been an eclectic mix of styles that was as offensive as the woman herself. Carla's ex-husband had been dating a senator, and the man's house had made the home and garden network at least once. It was tastefully decorated with modern colors in classic shapes, the sun deck a living room in its own right.

This estate put both of those to shame and possibly the president's house. I mean, it was massive and white and gaudy. Whatever sat before me was the perfect combination of craftsmen home and English cottage with floor to ceiling windows that would be a security nightmare and a stargazer's dream.

"I'm confused, though. If Mr. Kade turned in his father for attacking villages, why is he hiding? Why does he need to be kept hidden?" I asked. Internally, I was listing all the things I could claim to have witnessed to get an invitation. Unfortunately, most of the things I could claim had happened and were my fault... kind of.

Maybe I could get sent here on a "protect her from herself" assignment.

Or like... accidental suicide watch.

"His father and some of his more... devoted followers are missing." She maneuvered to a make-shift guard gate at the edge of the lawn. While there was a generator powered gate arm beside a portable guard shack, there was no fence or perimeter to keep people from going around on foot. "The people in the binder we showed you, all of them are known accomplices but they are constantly moving and have no link to the actual crimes. For better or worse, we cannot do more than watch them for now."

I let that sink in as I scanned the tree line to see if any barrier had been hidden behind it.

"Is a fence being delivered?" I asked, but the lines of caterers and stoic guards suggested this was it. Just a handful of people on a remote property with nothing but a plastic gate arm to keep people out. Winnie had impressive skills for search and detection, but she could only be in one place at a time and her ability to act as a fence was limited to how willing I was to order an attack. "Are more dogs coming?"

Carla measured her response, looking between me and the house itself while Winnie panted in my ear. It was confirmation that even she knew that she was a one and done attack dog. It was only fun to play chase and take down one baddie in a twenty-four period. Then she expected her treat, a squishy bed and a medal for distinguished service.

"How much did Cruz tell you about Conri Kade and tonight's fundraiser?"

We started to get out of the car. I adjusted my jacket and checked my gun in the shoulder holster. Carla was working something behind the wheel of the car while I stood in the open car door.

"Enough for me to think it's a trap. That anyone who insists a man in hiding show up for a large sum of money under the guise of philanthropy is just intending to lure him out to kill him," I shrugged as though people wanting to murder other people was an everyday occurrence. Satisfied with my weapon, I popped open the back door and let Winnie out. She hit the sand, stretched before shaking hard and smacking my leg with the straps of her vest. "I figured he either knew that and it was planned or he was too stupid to live."

"I'm not sure I like your cavalier attitude toward my life, Miss Sharp, but you are not wrong." The man who approached had the deep gravelly voice I'd heard during my call with Carla. I turned and took in the man I was most responsible for keeping un-blown-up. He was tall, extremely tall, and muscular in a way that didn't require supplements or enhancements. His dark skin was heavily contrasted by wearing beige linen pants, a beige tunic top with colorfully embroidered trim and a watch that cost more than my Jeep.

In a room full of tuxedos and suits, he would be a beacon for assault.

An assault I'd been brought on to thwart.

Why is nothing ever easy?

"Want to talk about cavalier attitude with your life? You've practically painted a target on your back in that outfit. You should have made it glow in the dark if you wanted to make it easy on them," I grumbled, Winnie shifting on her paws beside me. "Seriously, how am I supposed to help keep you alive when you look like the Dalai Lama's hot nephew went to a garden party for the queen?"

To my surprise, he barked out a laugh that carried through the night, sending shivers of pleasure through me. Mr. Cade did not disappoint on the promise his voice had made and I regretted missing our first meeting.

I'd miss his voice and his body more when he died.

"You are far more clever than most of my staff and the team guarding me. Perhaps the government should consider reinstating your status and stop trying to employ the easily manipulated. I imagine they had a hard time breaking you and I'd almost pay to have the opportunity to try it out for myself. I heard that your free spirit and creative thinking saved a lot of lives. Was making you submit really so important?"

"That's how the military works. Break you down, and build you up until you can work as a single unit with hundreds of others. A peacock amongst pigeons will always be an eyesore. Did they choose your outfit or are you noticeable on purpose?" I tried to keep my professionalism, but I was starting to question who had planned this whole event and whether or not we were predicted to survive.

If this was a suicide mission, I was taking my dog and my sister-in-law home.

The government could go suck an egg if they thought this was worth their lives.

"Yes, this outfit was chosen to draw attention as were you Miss Sharp. But I think between the two of us we can keep me alive."

"I'm not down to die in a game of mouse trap, Mr. Cade. Is there a plan to keep the distractions alive?" I challenged, waiting for him to answer while Carla held her breath beside me.

"Yes, Ms. Sharp. I'm rather fond of breathing and I can assure you only the best will be protecting both of us. Allow me to show you the interior, I think you'll find it satisfies more safety requirements than you think," his formal demeanor was a bit off putting. If I were honest, it was more likely due to my distaste for formality than the man himself.

He gestured for me to follow him and we ascended the stairs into a mansion bustling with caterers, servers, and party planners measuring the distance between tapered candlesticks. The room was a bustling nightmare of too many sounds, smells and inadequate lighting.

"What do you think, girl?" I whispered, wondering if she'd give me the excuse I needed to run away. "Anything explosive nearby?"

Winnie scented the air, flattening her ears and moving closer to my legs.

Not what I was expecting.

"Show me."

"What is wrong with your partner Miss Sharp?" He was watching her closely, her head tilted up and she looked to me for confirmation.

"It's OK, show me."

A small shriek came a hallway off to the left but she didn't react.

My eyebrows scrunched together and I gestured for everyone to follow Winnie. We went through three rooms and a parlor before arriving at a kitchen where a flurry of white coated men and women were rushing around the room.

My nose detected a few things that didn't smell appetizing, but nothing I would consider poison.

Winnie lifted her head, sniffing and moving slowly toward a pot half boiling on the stove. Whatever was inside had a surplus of vinegar, making the nauseating smell that filled the house, but she continued past it. For once in my beautiful partner's life, she even walked past a wooden charcuterie board without so much as a wayward nip in the direction of the cheese set out on it. We trailed behind her and when she sat down by a covered silver cold dish, I tilted my head. Winnie nudged my hand and I looked back at the bowl. Slowly, I peeled back the plastic wrap and tried to sniff it, coming up blank as to what the issue with it was. When I held it in front of Winnie, she pawed the edge, sending the bowl of cold noodles in mayo crashing to the floor. Her paws, digging through the mess, until she came to a stop when her claws scraped against something metal.

Confused, I grabbed a towel and wiped at the spot revealing the side of a metal container. I pried it open, surprised how soundlessly the hinges moved.

Almost like cold noodles were a natural lubricant.

Inside was a handgun and a small brick wrapped in grey plastic.

"Do you eat firearms, Mr. Kade?" I asked and he shook his head with a small frown. I held the box out for Carla and she frowned, lifting the gun out with a pen in the trigger guard.

"No..." He held the syllable longer than strictly necessary. I held the box out to Winnie so she could sniff the four inch by six inch brick.

She nosed it once, looked back at me and sat.

An irritated sigh escaped Carla and she dumped the gun in the sink before turning it on to clear the residue.

"Well, that clears everything up," she muttered, plucking the black handgun up with a towel. I offered her the box and she placed it on top of what was likely some sort of explosive. Conri Kade nodded his agreement before looking back at me.

"Miss Sharp, the goal tonight was to put myself out there as bait to hopefully capture my father and his followers. This whole facility has been swept and cleared numerous times by teams. I have been assured that they are the best and all safety and security precautions have been taken. I never expected you to find anything on my guests or those who come invited, it is all a ruse. You are here to draw attention and hopefully be distracting enough to keep me safe with your uncontrollable canine. But..." His eyes looked at the box, housing the gun and explosives, before shifting back to mine.

"But what?" I asked, tossing Winnie a treat for her find. Whatever was in that grey plastic brick was potent and I felt like maybe they should take it outside. Part of me wondered if the vinegar pot was to throw her off.

Another part of me thought the vinegar pot should possibly be used to discharge the explosives safely and save the world from whatever was boiling in there.

"They've already gotten in." Carla looked surprised and uncomfortable. It would appear the box was not a test of Winnie's skills. Someone managed to get a gun and device in the house and no one noticed.

"And now... now I fear you may be the only person here I can trust to keep me alive," he said quietly, and I felt a shiver of anxiety go through my body.

Chapter Nine: Performance Protocols

Once Winnie secured the exterior of the building, it was requested she search the inside as well. Despite my recommendation that another dog be brought in, Conri trusted Winnie alone with his safety. There had supposedly been other dogs and trained professionals who had swept the house and missed the small brick of explosives and gun in the bowl of pasta salad.

My instinct said it hadn't been in here when they searched. The instinct of everyone else was to place complete faith in us and disregard the previous sweeps. Winnie was the only one Conri felt confident could find any threats to his well-being.

Though I held the leash, I was acutely aware that I was unnecessary.

We began in the wine cellar, a surprisingly well stocked underground cave. For a place that didn't exist, there was a lot of money sitting underneath it gathering dust. Conri offered me something bottled the same year I was born with a label in French, but I declined when I realized I didn't have cargo pockets to put it in.

Carla opted to put it in the car for me while Winnie and I moved upstairs.

The first floor had a living room, a dining room, a parlor, six toilets in 4 bathrooms (a mystery we didn't want to look into) and a coat closet the size of my apartment. During our tour, Winnie located three concealed stashes of Girl Scout cookies, four bags of beef jerky and a wheel of cheese that may or may not have been aging on purpose.

Hidden intermittently were single bullets, they were of all calibers and in various degrees of corrosion. Given that the mansion didn't exist, I suspected these were strays lost by previous resident's security teams, but at least three matched the gun we'd found in the kitchen.

On the floor above, we found two service workers engaged in recreational horizontal cardio. A mood that was immediately ruined for them when Winnie stuck her nose into the connection point and one of them started screaming.

Respectfully, I kept my back to the whole scene while politely requesting they wash their hands before touching any food.

There were at least ten more bathrooms, including the en-suites attached to all eight bedrooms. Each one had a bathtub that could double as a swimming pool and an empty gun safe mounted behind the toilets.

"Whoever built this house was paranoid," I told Winnie and she wiggled her brows with a soft snort. "I mean, they're here because their lives are in danger. I get that, but why put a gun safe by the toilet? I mean the whole caught with your pants down thing is a metaphor. Who is legitimately scared of that?"

My partner stuck her nose in the slightly ajar door and sneezed. The force startled her and she let out a fart that stole all breathable oxygen from the room.

"Oh my dog, why?" I gasped, bursting back into the bedroom and hitting the ventilation fan. "Put your butt in a wall safe and the entire world would be safer."

Staggering to the bedroom window, I shoved it up and thrust my head out into the deepening darkness. The fundraising party was scheduled to begin at ten in the evening and I marveled that not only could a party start that late, but people would actually attend something that started at the same time I went to bed.

They were either dedicated partiers or I was old.

There was no need for philanthropy to get in the way of sleeping in the digital age. You could electronically transfer funds to anyone, anywhere in your pajamas. Who gets dressed up and goes outside to give strangers money anymore?

Just beyond the tree line, a bright light summoned my attention like a bat signal in the woods. If I weren't at the premier party for people who did not exist, I would think it was held over there.

Curiosity and a desire for fresh air won out over my sense of duty. I pulled out my cheap cell phone and launched the maps app, zooming in and out on my estimation of where the lights were located.

There was nothing there.

No matter how much I expanded the image, the only thing that appeared in the green blob was a trail head with a small parking lot. There looked to be a large roadway and a few small businesses, the nearest of which were two farm houses six miles away according to the legend. None of the business names populated, nor did the addresses of the homes. The only point of interest that was labeled was...

"Brave Heart Trail?" I said, looking down at Winnie. I'd heard the name recently, but I couldn't place it. Zooming in closer, I found a fire road that meandered to the side of the trail, but at some point it just ended in a patch of green pixels and grey squares that refused to identify themselves.

I grumbled at the device and the Internet as a whole before switching from the lighted house to the light of the stars peeking out through the night sky.

"What are you doing, chica?"

I jumped from my skin and slammed my head against the window frame.

"Damnit, Cruz!" I shouted, barely holding onto my cell phone as I pulled my head back into the house. I used my other hand to rub the sore spot and wondered how I could give him a matching lump on his head. "I could have killed you!"

"Winnie's gas isn't nearly as effective after you open the window, Cyn," he laughed, crouching down to give my dog some love. Her eyes went to me first, as though verifying he wasn't on the list of men who deserved to be eliminated from the face of the earth.

I shrugged at her.

"Your choice. I'm done with all of them."

Her eyebrows wiggled and she sat on his foot. He rubbed the soft spot at the base of her ears, and she melted into a boneless puddle. I searched within myself for signs of jealousy or annoyance, but I had nothing.

I really was just done with all of it.

"All of who, chica?" Ian's voice held affection, his eyes soft as he studied my furry friend. When she pawed at the hand petting her, Ian switched from rubbing her ears to rubbing her exposed belly.

"Doesn't matter. Is it time?" I asked, checking my gun in its holster for the tenth time. It had been a long time since I had been armed and I wasn't sure the feeling of carrying it would ever be compared to riding a bike.

"Yes, they are opening the gate." His voice was soft and I glanced his way to find him staring. My eyes narrowed, challenging him, but he didn't look away.

"What? You know it's rude to stare, right?" I blinked at him but when he remained silent, I was the first to turn away. Instead of waiting, I tapped my leg twice and Winnie bolted upright and took her place beside me as I exited the room and scanned the hallway. We'd made it through all of the rooms and the top floor was officially clear of weapons and snacks.

"I can smell burning, Cyn," he whispered against my ear and a warm tingle shuddered through me, forcing me to whip around and face him. "You're overthinking."

"I am not," I said, shoving him to gain a few inches of personal space.

He didn't move.

"No?" He traced his index finger along the line of my chin until he reached my lips and traced first the bottom and then the top.

My stomach fluttered and I nearly moaned.

Apparently, I was not done with *that* part of spending time with men.

That was still very appealing, and Cruz had proven to have potential in that department. Potential pleasure, potential disaster... his potential was endless.

Like all reactions without enough energy, however, I couldn't find a catalyst to kick start the reaction. Our kinetic energy remained the same, but we never reached the threshold potential.

"No." It came out breathy and I cleared my throat to try again. Despite his potential, I had work to do. "I'm intentionally not thinking. Thinking is bad, we are on autopilot."

I stepped away and Winnie followed, joining my descent toward the steady hum of voices.

"Are we still on the gate?" I asked, not daring to turn around as I made my way down to the second-floor landing and taking the short hallway to the first-floor staircase. The whole place looked like it belonged in that David Bowie movie with staircases to nowhere and everywhere all at once.

It was a miracle I didn't need breadcrumbs to find my way back.

Mostly because Winnie would have eaten them and I'd still be lost.

Cruz wrapped a warm arm around my waist and pressed my back against his front.

"Do you want to be on the gate? Or do you want to be on something else?" His lips were brushing against the spot just below my ear and my lady parts let out a growl of desire. We had been here before, he and I.

Been here and been left wanting.

Somehow, none of that stopped the wanting. Not now, not then... he was like an itch I needed to scratch to move on.

"I..." my voice stopped working when his thumb made a slow circle on my hip and I rested my head on his shoulder behind me. Being tough was exhausting. Maybe for just one minute, I could be weak.

Just one minute.

"You?" He was amused. I wanted to hit him but I also wanted to jump on top of him and...

"Cynthia, there you are." My eyes snapped open to make visual contact with Conri who was checking his phone. "You will no longer be screening guests at the gate. I'd like you and Winnie..."

He stopped suddenly, looking at me for the first time. Whatever he had been doing on the device concluded, he'd passed it back to an assistant and was giving me his full attention. His assistant gave a slight smirk and disappeared with the phone in her hand.

I was still wrapped in Ian's arms and my face was warm even under the air conditioning. While the pound of hair spray keeping my bun in place was probably doing its job, and my suit hadn't been molested, I felt like a woman doing the walk of shame.

"Am I interrupting something?" He cocked a single eyebrow, and I elbowed Cruz backward. He took in a sharp breath and released me.

"No, sir. Where would you like us?"

His eyes danced between me and the man who I could hear chuckling behind me.

"Probably not the same place he would but I appreciate your dedication to your responsibilities. Cruz knows where he belongs, and hopefully he can refrain from getting distracted again. I'd like you and your partner in whatever room I'm in. Nothing overt, you can linger on the periphery, but I'd like you within 'sniffing' distance, if Sgt. Pupperson will pardon the pun," he winked at her, and I felt my head tilt. "You two are internationally famous. Not knowing her name would be a crime."

Hesitating, I wasn't sure I believed him but couldn't find a reason not to. Winnie's disaster videos were known far and wide, but her rank and title were rarely included.

"Her name is attached to her flank in Velcro though I'm curious why a canine would need armor for a security detail. I've also had men visit your office and confirmed her name on the window matches the one you've stuck to her vest. You... piqued my curiosity." His answer offered no reference to time, but for it to be fresh in his mind gave me an idea.

"Are your men still at my office? Why aren't they here helping keep you safe?" Ian stilled behind me and I wondered if he wanted the answer to my question or if he knew the answer and was waiting to see how Conri would respond. There was no way his men had been at my office this week, since I'd been at my office. Learning faces and killing time, waiting for tonight with my marching orders and a broken heart... Orders which were to stay stationary beside a gate.

Which meant they were either there now or he had been planning this party longer than I'd been invited to it.

"Again, your clever mind..." he was speaking mostly to himself. "Yes. After your discovery, I doubted the people in my employ. They have been with me for some time, and while nothing tragic has befallen me, someone has had a bit more information than they should. All of my men joined from my home country, they'd have known my father and his men before the treaty and war crimes came into play. My suspicions were raised, and I took this opportunity for misdirection to test their loyalty. I hope you don't mind, but they were encouraged to go inside."

"Whatever. If any of the coffee in my space is missing after they leave, I'm going to retroactively refuse to help you find that gun," I huffed down the stairs as he offered me another look of amused questioning. "I said what I said."

Cruz chuckled softly behind me, and Winnie butted Mr. Kade's hand with her head.

"I am starting to think you will make a terrible shadow," he extended his palm against the top of her head and rubbed gently. "But I'd like you with me anyway. I will take personal responsibility for any coffee you report missing and replace it accordingly."

Two hours had passed and no one had attempted to murder Mr. Kade.

He'd drank, shaken hands, smiled and rubbed elbows with people who smelled like Hollister and Abercrombie got jiggy in a whorehouse. The smell was legendary and awful, sending Winnie into a sneezing fit as a dull throb pounded behind my right eye. Every fake laugh sent another blast through my skull, every condescending compliment tossed casually at the servers and wait staff made my blood boil.

Also, Mr. Kade had been drinking for hours and he still hadn't gone pee.

What sort of inhuman creature puts up with these people without so much as a pee break for solitude?

"Do you need a break?" Cruz asked and I nodded.

Thank dog someone remembered I was human.

"So does Winnie, but he's depending on her nose."

I took his presence as an invitation to close my eyes for a moment without fear of it being the exact second my charge would become hideously dismembered.

"I think you two can take ten without the world coming to an end. Not like this is a pretzel statue in Germany. Mr. Kade would be significantly harder to squish." His slight dig was accompanied by a gentle tap on my butt.

"You must really like it when I punch you in the face. Not only do you keep pushing me, you also want to repeat the crimes of others to see if there will be a different reaction," I smirked, but moved toward the door. "If I would kill a man's pretzel stature for touching my butt, don't think I won't hurt your pretty face."

"Aww... you think I'm pretty."

I snickered but didn't turn around. The sounds of wealth and condescension were heavier than the perfumes and Winnie lead us to freedom through a partially open glass slider. A white wooden balcony with a wide railing beckoned me forward.

"Wow," I breathed, and I could hear Winnie's silent agreement.

Though some of the guests had spilled out onto the wooden deck, the vast forest dimmed their chatter. A sea of trees stretched into the night, the bright moon casting everything in a romantic glow.

Perfect for alien abductions or a rogue werewolf attack.

Winnie led the way to a set of steps, and we moved quietly to the grass below. The house screamed hedge maze or sculpture garden, but the humble lawn was a reminder that this place technically didn't exist.

We moved farther into the night. When all that remained was the scent of pine, I took my first deep breath. During my exhale, Winnie let out a loud string of barks that shook the night.

"What the hell-" my voice drowned out under her raucous alert and my eyes scanned the area.

Just beyond the west tree line, something moved.

"Crap," I activated the phone in my pocket and approached the area casually. Still on her leash, Winnie was practically dragging me forward. "Crap, I think there's someone in the tree line. Keep the phone open."

I shouted into the headphones, keeping my posture calm and casual. When no one responded, I touched the phone in my pocket but I couldn't take it out without giving away my position. I pulled the headphones out and tossed the set down in the grass. Ten feet out, the figure froze and I had a split second to register the reflection of the moonlight on the silver weapon before I hauled Winnie to the ground.

Muzzle flash bathed the area in harsh light and the shot ringing in my ears shattered the silence of the night.

In a moment everything was thrown into chaos.

Chapter Ten: Goose Chase

"Come on girl," I shouted over the ringing in my ears. Pulling my firearm from its holster, I took off toward the tree line at a dead sprint. I was aiming to intercept a man fleeing toward the house, even as I lost sight of him in the dark. His outfit was tactical black with cargo pockets and when my eyes failed, I trusted my ears.

The man was just to my right and coming in fast.

I shifted to redirect my inertia, but my angle was off by a few degrees and I found myself behind him. With another burst of leg strength, I launched myself toward his back, catching him around the waist and pressing on the back of his knees.

We crashed to the ground, the man rolling over so I was on top of him, face up. I ripped off the ski mask that covered his face while his arms smacked at my torso.

He was one of the men in the binder Carla had shown me but I blanked on if he was in the friend or foe binder.

Femi something I thought, his elbow catching me in the ribs as he fought to get me off his chest. The gun flew from my hand and I lost it in the darkness. My hands grappled for purchase against his flailing arms, his knee connecting with my diaphragm and knocking the air from my lungs. In the split second it took to recover, Femi had transitioned so that his legs straddled my body, fists poised to attack.

"Take him out," I shouted, dodging the attacks but growing dizzier by the moment.

Winnie darted forward, sinking her teeth into his thigh and tugging. Femi screamed, his frame turning to address Winnie. I used the brief distraction to shove him backward.

He lost his balance, Winnie tugging on his leg released the clamp-like grip. I wiggled out, kneeing him in the crotch with a satisfied smirk at his screaming.

Two more figures emerged from the woods.

"Two more," I shouted, hoping my phone hadn't disconnected in the scuffle. Fighting my way back to standing, I left Winnie to her chomping and surged toward another target.

This one was slower, but he had more weight and I went low. As I made contact, a large van rounded the building, pieces of the gate arm stuck in the grill.

It was dark blue and on a mission to mow down the people on the grass lawn.

Armed guards ran behind the van, none of them firing on the moving vehicle. Behind the wheel, I could see the driver applying pressure to his arm. Either he had been shot or cut on his left arm breaching the entry gate, blood was seeping through his fingers while his face was screwed in painful concentration.

"Cyn! Get down!"

My body dropped and a shot rang over my head as I registered the instruction came from Carla. A thud preceded a whoosh of air and a heavy weight settled beside me.

It didn't move.

"Winnie!" I jumped to my feet and searched out her form. "Winnie, place!"

Her jingling collar clattered as she approached me and sat beside me. A small amount of blood was on her lip, a small strip of fabric caught in her incisor. On the ground beside us was another man in all black. The van barreled toward us, fishtailing in the damp grass as it tried to change directions.

"Run!" I ordered Winnie, noting that no more men were coming from the woods but two were rushing the now obliterated gate. Armed gate guards opened fire and the intruders took cover, firing back.

From inside the house, a high pitched scream pierced the air and glass shattered. A slow moving stampede of people in expensive clothing had started pouring through the main entrance, screaming and shouting at the gun fight happening on the lawn.

"Let's go Winnie!"

We took off toward the back of the house, Winnie leading the way. Her floppy tongue was lolling out of the side of her mouth. The van was following us, but it got bogged down by a mass of guards who had patrolled the interior, arriving to fight the group in black camo. It was too much chaos and though I knew not all of them had come out of the woods, I couldn't find a massive tunnel they popped up from, either.

Every man was engaged, the van halted looking for a new path and I pushed my feet to return to the patio. The numbers were too much, we needed to get back to Conri.

Twenty yards from the back patio, my eye's alighted on a white clad figure seeming to float in midair. I hesitated, Winnie slowing beside me reflexively. While the floating sack of potatoes would have been a cool magic trick, I had a bad feeling I was looking at something else.

The van's headlights lit the patio and confirmed my biggest fear of the moment. Conri Kade was thrown over a man's shoulder, being carried down the steps from the back patio. Beneath him, the man was dressed in black from head to toe, another ski mask obscuring any chance I had to identify the abductor.

Winnie scented the air and let out a growl.

"Go get him back," I ordered, and she kicked her speed up another notch. The man had escaped the wooden staircase from the patio, searching wildly for... his eyes met the van and he turned. Two furry paws slammed into his back, sending him forward and Mr. Kade's body flopping to the ground in front of him.

Winnie took up a guard position, snarling at the man as he tried to get back on his feet.

"Leave it! We'll try again!" The driver of the van threw open the door and Mr. Kade's would-be captor sprinted toward the open door.

"Winnie, protect! Don't let anyone but Cruz or Carla near him!" I shouted and she lowered into a dangerous prowl. Despite years of training, I had no real knowledge as to how my dog understood such specific instructions. The "protect" one was obvious, but I knew in my bones she would only let Ian or Carla near the fallen man. This fact above all others sent my feet toward the van.

Our only hope to avoid a repeat was to capture all of them.

Once the man who had been carrying Conri got to the van, the driver started fighting the muddy grass to get momentum. The failed kidnapper leapt into the moving vehicle, slamming the door as a sheet of mud sprayed behind the van and coated my already bloody outfit. My sleeve wiped the worst of it from my eyes and my vision cleared enough to see the silver ladder leading to the roof at the rear of the van just behind the driver. With a flying leap, I grasped a rung and held tight, feet dragging until my arms got the strength to move up a rung.

Feet firmly on the bumper, mud splashing behind me, I held tight as the van reversed direction. The fighting at the gate had reached a conclusion, bodies littering the ground in both injury and death. With no defenses, the van rolled over the plastic remnants of the gate arm onto the hard-packed dirt road.

There were no windows on the rear of the van, but I kept toward the center to avoid the side mirrors. Dust kicked up and small rocks pelted my legs, but they had already gone numb from the adrenaline dump. Even without the mud, my sweaty palms would have struggled to hold on, but I refused to let my hands let up.

White knuckle grip, I felt when the road beneath our tires changed from dirt to asphalt. While the ride became smoother, the van picked up speed and I pressed my body against the van ladder to reduce drag. Terrified of falling, I peeled my fingers from the side bar one hand at a time, wrapping the arm around the frame in a bear hug. I locked my grip on the opposite elbow and leaned my head against the rail.

"We're on the roadway," I tried speaking with my face toward my pocket. "The moon is behind the van, but I can't tell the direction from here."

My voice was lost to my own ears but I had to hope the sensitive microphone could catch what my damaged ears could not. The van activated a blinker and I chanced a glance beside me.

We were turning left.

The vehicle slowed, and the van arced wide. It bumped over a steep inclined curb and I didn't adjust quickly enough. Inertia pulled me into the turn, putting pressure on my already exhausted forearms. My grip gave out and I toppled to the side, barrel rolling across the asphalt trying to protect my neck. The thin suit material gave easily, tearing and scraping the skin underneath.

"Ow," I muttered quietly, back on the ground facing up at the stars. Wherever we'd gone had more light pollution. There weren't as many celestial bodies sparkling in the sky and the ones I could see weren't nearly as calming with the shouting coming from whatever building sat behind me.

"I'm dead," I whispered. Then I wiggled my fingers and toes, correcting my earlier statement.

"I wish I were dead."

That sentiment also felt wrong and I sat up.

The world spun and my eyes clamped shut to keep from falling over again and vomiting. Keeping them shut, I found my feet and staggered toward the noise, sticking my hand in my pocket to grab my phone.

My fingers closed around the rectangular pocket computer and I plucked it out, glancing quickly at the screen to see it shattered but still powered on with a call active. I used it to shine light around the parking lot and determined it was not well maintained and had a few too many wet spots for an area that hadn't had rain in weeks.

"Oh thank dog," I whispered, just as a car horn blasted, nearly splitting my brain box in two. My hands clamped against my ears, dropping everything to keep the two hemispheres joined at the amygdala.

The horn blared again and I stumbled onto a sidewalk. So far, my head was still in one piece, and so was the phone I dropped though it landed in one of the liquid collection divots and I was not sure it would be sanitary. A large green vehicle with a diesel engine rumbled by, Garth Brooks screaming from the cab, loud and proud.

A sickening crunch muted all the other sounds in the area.

"That bastard!" I whisper cried, the cell phone I'd bought mere days ago, now completely obliterated in a puddle of pee. "Ugh."

Fighting the urge to sob, I took a moment to gather myself before straightening to look around. I was in fact on a sidewalk that sat under a brown wooden awning. The old barn style building had neon signs featuring alcohol brands and acronyms I could only translate to mean *sports*.

The blue van wasn't parked in front of the establishment.

Keeping a hand against the wall, I staggered to the rear of the building. On the way, I passed a couple making out, two dumpsters and a man in a white apron urinating against what was probably the electric meter.

"That's a piss-poor idea," I snickered to myself, but the dirty look he shot me indicated it wasn't quiet enough. "Sorry, brain injury."

He flipped me off and stomped into a door marked "Employees Only".

"Definitely not eating here."

I made it around to the rear and found the blue van parked against a chain link fence. Even from here, it was obviously empty. Every door stood open, a set of fresh tire tracks painted in rubber leaving from the front of the van's parking spot.

"Damn it," I whispered and reached for my phone to have someone come search the van.

Only I still didn't have a phone.

"Crap, I have to go into the bar," I whispered, pressing my head against the side of the building.

Then pulled it back as the whiff of urine and deep-fried poison got stronger. Turning slowly, I traced the wall back to the front door and stopped, staring blankly at it for a few moments longer than was strictly necessary to determine if the door was push or pull.

Particularly since the air flow showed it swung both ways and I was being a baby.

"Deep breath, Sharp," I whispered, shoving on the door and taking a step inside.

If this were a movie, there would have been a record scratch as a dozen pairs of eyes locked onto me. I could only imagine what I looked like, covered in mud, blood and road rash from falling off a van. Normally, I would stare them all down, but today was not the day to start a fight.

I'd already been in several and my body was declaring me the loser.

Ignoring all of them, I stumbled to the long wooden bar to see a large man with a face obscured by the hair growing out of it. He was wearing jeans and a plaid flannel, while behind him a slightly damaged flatscreen TV showed a sport where people glided back and forth on a field of white with sticks.

Either there was a fly on the screen, or the sticks were for hitting a small black dot.

"Last Call is in five minutes, order quick," he gruffed and I shook my head.

"No money. Can I borrow your phone?" My own voice was strained and foreign to my ears. He gave me a long look and I blinked back at him indifferently. "Please?"

"Why should I let you borrow my phone?" He smirked beneath his beard that potentially had its own beard growing beneath it. Despite the feminine connotations, his beard was both voluminous and silky.

"Because..." I didn't have time to come up with a response. The whole building shook and a loud popping sound drowned out the sound of the televisions gracing most of the walls.

"What the hell was that?" He looked bewildered, patrons sloshing drinks as they looked around for signs of danger. When none was immediately present, they looked for a remote to turn up the TV.

Apparently, one needed to hear the stick hitting the dot in order to enjoy it.

The barback came in through the kitchen door, looking enthusiastically horrified at whatever he had witnessed. Seeing him in the slightly brighter indoors, I was horrified at the droplets beading on his shoes, partially undone fly, and the same dirt smudge I'd seen on his hand in the alley.

If I knew any health inspectors, I'd call them immediately.

"The... the..."

I plopped on a barstool, pressing my face against the filthy plank that was both sticky and slippery.

"Let me guess?" I muttered into the surface. "The blue van just blew up."

Chapter Eleven: Maple Blasted

"The fire truck still isn't here!" Beardy complained, but I had a feeling every local and regional emergency service in the area was caught up in the incident at the safe house. While nothing had been on fire when I left, the chances were pretty good that something had caught fire.

Fire often followed planned attacks in my experience.

It also followed unplanned attacks and accidental international incidents.

Frankly, it was just always safest to assume there was fire.

"My brother hasn't called back either," I grumbled, eliciting a stink eye from Beardy. "What? The van wasn't parked near anything flammable. It'll burn itself out soon enough. But if I don't change clothes before my scabs stop bleeding, they'll start drying into a crust with fibers from my clothing embedded in them so I have to tear them back open to get the stupid fabric out. My need for assistance is greater than yours, whether you and the national emergency people agree or not."

Beardy gave me a stern look but didn't argue.

I was granted access to the coveted bar landline once the van blew up and I promised I wasn't calling the trigger device on another one. The bar phone was so old, it had a cord and was mounted to the wall outside the employees only bathroom. It didn't have a rotary dial, but it was still on par with Alexander Graham Bell era technology.

Waiting for Seth to pick up, I peeked my head into the employee bathroom to see if there was some sort of sewage back up that would prevent use. I saw a mop and a bucket, sitting beside a sink and a hole in the ground that had either lost it's toilet or never had one.

Still didn't justify peeing in the alley, but who was I to judge those with an outie when I was limited by my innie.

I listened to Seth's voicemail with the enthusiasm of a generation who only memorized a few numbers from the "before" times. With cell phones, no one had had to memorize a phone number in the past decade. My brother had gotten a cell phone before me, and I'd memorized his number for emergencies. His number hadn't changed since high school and calling him would be the fastest way to reach Carla. Unfortunately, he was part of the "generation who does not answer unknown callers", but I left a message with my location, details of the van's whereabouts and disposition as well as the bar's name and a recommendation to Google the phone number as I hadn't been given the number. The message assured him I was fine, but Carla would need all that information... and to come get me.

That had been fifteen minutes ago and he hadn't called back. I'd even made sure to let him know his wife was well and alive the last I'd seen her. Part of me worried the phone's ringer was broken, he'd called back but I wasn't notified because the phone hadn't been serviced since the Reagan Administration.

Then it rang with a prank caller asking about running refrigerators and I admitted defeat.

The only logical conclusion was he hadn't listened to the message.

He'd probably ignored it thinking I wanted him to renew his auto warranty.

Or Sylvia had demolished the family home with him inside and I was now without any male siblings.

"How much experience do you have with vehicle fires and scabs?" Beardy was studying me closely. I tried to give him a warm smile, but all I managed was a toothy grimace. Must have been the awkward tooth display that gave me away. "You look familiar."

Not flattering after that facial expression.

"Only if you have the Internet and watch pointless videos. Picture me with a German shepherd mix, standing in front of something demolished, covered in something unsanitary and..." I caught sight of my reflection in the mirror behind the bar. "Meh, this is actually a little better than I look in those videos."

My hair had stayed in its bun and aside from the addition of a few bits of gravel, grass and dead bugs, it looked the same as when I'd placed it there before leaving my apartment. Probably I should send a positive letter to the hair gel company's quality control department. The suit was ripped and stained, but it still covered my whole body and none of the blood on the outside was mine.

All my injuries were bleeding onto the other side.

A blessing when coated in the blood of a stranger. Especially after being forced to learn about bloodborne pathogens, though the porous nature of fabric meant it was actually as useless as being naked if I didn't change soon.

A short glass with amber liquid appeared in front of me and I looked back at Beardy.

"If your night was anything like what I've seen in those videos, you need that," he tapped the counter and sauntered away toward the rear of the bar to check on the flaming van. Beside me, a man in flannel hadn't broken his gaze from the ice sport game with sticks and I studied him as I threw back the contents of my glass.

Last call had come and gone and the rest of the bar had filed out. The only people remaining were the two employees and the man sitting next to me.

"Are you Canadian?" I asked, deciding to make the most of my detour.

"What's it to you?" He didn't spare me a glance and I considered how to phrase my question. Was asking people if they were Canadian a social faux pas or was he just grouchy? I knew better than to ask a woman with a belly if she was pregnant, but Canadian was hardly an insult.

They didn't elect a narcissist and provided adequate warning about moose.

Mooses?

Meece?

"Line of inquiry?" I offered, feeling a flush creep into my face as the liquor hit my stomach. "Geez, what the hell was that?"

Beardy reappeared and looked at my glass.

"Catastrophe Chick can drink," he commented, pouring me another. "You were right about the van. Fire burned itself out and still no sign of emergency services. The Blades might beat the Ice Dogs in the CHL Memorial Cup before they get here."

He snickered to himself while the man beside me let out a tooth baring snarl.

I shot back the new drink, my head already feeling light and floaty after the first one. Most of my healing scrapes faded into background pinpricks, and I had already forgotten the bruises from tackling a man and falling off the back of a moving vehicle.

"Is that ice stick sport trash talk?" I asked and there was a noticeable slur.

"Hockey," my neighbor grunted.

"Right... but... not American hockey? Because you're Canadian?" Every syllable was thick, but I tried to watch the little black dot fly across the screen.

"Why are you so fixated on Canadians?" Beardy was watching me with narrowed eyes and I tried to squint at him.

"I lost one. Well, I didn't lose one, someone else lost one. I'm trying to figure out what Canadian men like so I know where to start looking or what to leave a trail of for him to find his way home. He could have just wandered away. Just because someone wanted him smuggled here doesn't mean he wanted to be here... he could have gotten distracted by ice stick sports and flaming vans and..."

Beardy and Neighbor shared a knowing look.

"You guys found a lost Canadian?" I asked, practically squealed, clapping my hands together. "Now we can give him back! Where is he? Can I see him?"

"Who told you about my brother?" Neighbor asked and I blinked at his face.

"Your brother?" I asked, some of the floaty feelings dissipating. "You're related to Robin and Noah? And you took him from a pregnant lady?"

I slurred the last part in my best *tsk tsk* voice.

"What? Who's Noah?" Beardy poured me another glass while popping the cap off a bottle of beer for the man beside me. Apparently after Last Call, drinks were free.

Maybe it was only illegal to sell after 2AM but not drink after it.

"Noah is my missing Canadian. Did you also lose a Canadian brother man person?" I considered the liquid in the glass and counted back the hours since I'd last eaten. It was a reasonably bad idea to drink it, but one might argue it was medicinal.

One might also argue that taping a traffic cone to a horse proved the existence of unicorns.

I wasn't in the mood to argue with either of those people, so I took my shot and set the glass back down.

"Yeah, my brother. I was working on getting him a place here but there were some issues with documents and paperwork. It got pretty confusing and I heard about this company that helps mountain men immigrate here. Real sweet old lady ran it, named Pearl. But a week past when she promised he'd arrive, he still wasn't here. When I called the number, it was disconnected. Website, email, every contact method I'd used was useless and everyone back home assured me he'd left with most of his belongings," my neighbor stopped and chugged the beer in front of him. "Except he never got here and he never went home."

"Was your brother supposed to visit on a tourist visa?" I asked, wishing I had something to take notes on for when I forgot this in the morning. My eyes scanned the bar and I saw a pen holding a man bun in place behind Beardy's head. Without permission, I plucked it from his hair and stole the spiral notebook I'd spotted in his back pocket.

"Smooth, Catastrophe Chick. If you wanted to cop a feel, you could have asked," Beardy snickered and I offered him a view of my middle finger.

"What is his name, occupation and area of origin?"

"I didn't use a Visa, I paid in cash. His name is John Jack Johnson and he worked in the lumber mills up in Saskatchewan," he let out a loud burp and I sat back from the smell.

"OK, so he's... a lumberjack? From the mountains?" I hedged my bets, hoping lumber mills encompassed the phrase lumberjack. "Did he have a phone when he left? Have you tried calling him?"

"He ain't a lumberjack. He shapes and treats the wood, processing it for lumber sales and distribution. It's pretty physically demanding, but he liked to work his muscles. Kept him popular with the ladies," Mr. Johnson eyed me from top to bottom and I reflexively made a gagging sound. "As far as a phone, he said cell phones were fryin' everyone's brain and it was best not to have one."

I rubbed at my temples and tried to work through what two mountain men without cell phones would do if they found themselves in America.

Probably find the nearest sheep.

I gagged at my own thought and shoved it aside.

"This... Pearl you mentioned, did you ever hear anything in the background when you talked with her? Anything that might have given you an idea of what she did or where she was?" I scribbled notes on Beardy's order pad, but there wasn't much to jot down. "Did you meet her in person? Did she offer any personal details or anecdotes?"

"Any what now? She didn't poison me, she was just trying to help me get my brother over here," he scoffed at my question.

"Not *antidote*, anecdote. Stories or memories that might make her recognizable if you saw her in person?" He blinked at me, hand in a white-knuckle grip on his beer.

"I heard something," the man in the apron pushed out into the main bar area and I got my first half-decent look at his face.

He was short and stocky, but his face had a boyish charm accentuated with dimples and a slight cleft in his chin.

There was also still dirt on his hands and he was drying a glass with a rag.

"Richie here was searching for a pen to write down where the money was supposed to be sent and he handed me the phone to make sure it didn't hang up. While he was gone, there was a woman in the background shouting about how there was no way at her age she could make her own lube and all the foreplay in the world wasn't going to make that dildo go in," his boyish looks faded with the perverted smirk.

"You heard that? Another time he was on the line I could hear a woman shouting at a supplier of 'uppers' for not bringing enough. Only professionals kept it going that long without assistance," Beardy puzzled on his words and I tilted my head at him. "I just thought that she was sellin' meth. Happens out here. But now with what he said... think she was talkin' about penis pills?"

I nodded and looked at the notepad.

John Johnson, lube, dildos, uppers/penis pills, Pearl, cell phones bad, cash not Visa.

"Damn," I grumbled, grabbing the glass and throwing back what I'd just learned was whiskey. "I'm going to need a few more of these to get through the next half hour of my life."

Shoving up from my bar stool, I started to walk toward the "employee restroom". My foot caught on Neighbor's stool and I fell forward into his lap.

Face first.

It twitched under my face and I pretended to bite his crotch area, forgetting briefly he was a complete stranger with a missing family member. I so rarely got to harass men in public anymore and it was easy to remember why I thought it was so fun.

Until his lap started getting firmer under my face.

"Hehe, just met the main johnson of the Johnson family," I snickered into the slight bulge in the front of his jeans. Sober me would have tried to figure out if it was a grower or a shower, but drunk me just wanted to watch him squirm. "I wonder if this johnson needs uppers."

My cackle was followed by a firm hand around my arm pulling me back upright.

"Thanks, Big Johnson. I wasn't against meeting Little Johnson but it's not a great time. I have dried blood caked on my clothes, a lot of bruises and I'm du-runk!"

Big Johnson gave a curt nod, but his cheeks were tinted pink under all that flannel.

"What's happening in the next half hour that you have to drink more?" The barback asked, and I blinked at him touching a bottle of tequila.

"Don't touch that! I know you haven't washed your hands since pissing outside," I warned, watching Beardy snatch the bottle from him and pointing stiff armed toward the kitchen. He grabbed a pouch of antibacterial wipes from beneath the counter and wiped down the bottle, the counter and everything near where Apron Man had been standing. "Do you have to sterilize a lot when that man works?"

He nodded, then he poured me another drink and picked up his stolen notebook to check my scribbled list.

"None of this looks helpful," he pointed out, but I shook my head.

"That's where you're wrong, Beardy," I threw back the fresh drink and steeled myself for the call I was about to make. "If you have senior citizens and sex toys this close to Sweat Pea, you have a lead. If you have a lead, you can follow it, whether you want to or not. In this case, I do not want to follow this one but it's not really about me, so I'll make the call. Coincidentally, it's one of the only other phone numbers I memorized. I was going to call my best friend since my brother sucks Little Johnson's, but this is as good a time as any to ask questions and find a lift home. Maybe I can get her to spring for more alcohol so I can black out after asking about her sex life."

The cackle that escaped was tinged with desperation and fear.

"Who is this *she* you're going to call?" John Johnson's brother was making a concentrated effort not to look at me after I'd had my face in his lap and I nearly giggled as the fourth shot worked its way into my system.

"The leader of the senior swingers and most prominent connoisseur of porn in my town," I sighed, holding onto the counter as I moved closer to the phone. "Helpful in this situation because she's also my mother and she can either come get me or send someone."

Mouth hanging open, Beardy poured me a fifth shot.

"Lynn Sharp is your mom?" I almost fell over reaching behind me for my new shot. Beardy knowing my mother was so far from a good thing I was considering pouring the shot in my eyes to burn out the image before remembering I hadn't seen anything.

With a curt nod, I downed the shot and started toward the phone again.

"Godspeed, Catastrophe Chick," he gave a mock salute, so I offered him a single finger, my favorite one that was right in the middle.

Chapter Twelve: Burn Out

I've gone blind, I thought, my eyes opening to complete darkness.

I reached my arm out beside me, carefully tapping the soft surface. When I didn't immediately feel anything, I held my breath to listen.

One heartbeat.

Two heartbeats.

My throat constricted and my head went fuzzy, forcing me to choke out a breath and gasp for air. This led to a coughing fit and any chance I had of a stealth awakening was thwarted when the coughing turned into a juicy hack with full body spasms.

"Sit. Drink." Someone appeared beside me, pushing me into a seated position and forcing the straw of a sippy cup into my mouth. While common sense said not to drink anything put into your mouth when you were blind, confused and in absolute darkness, I hadn't any common sense left.

My lips closed around the straw and I started sucking up the fluid. It tasted like water and my greedy throat gulped down every drop until the hollow sound of sucking filled the room.

"Not sure if I should be impressed or jealous, chica," the cup moved away and I felt the rough pads of Cruz's fingertips brush along my face. "You look like hell."

"Winnie?" I croaked out and a heavy thump dipped the bed beside me. Reaching out a hand, I made contact with her soft fur and let out a breath I hadn't realized I was holding.

Like a romance novel heroine, I would give up breathing before giving up the person I loved.

Even if that person was a dog.

Sensing my need, Winnie snuggled closer until her weight was a comforting pressure on my chest. With her affection, I settled and worked to remember what had happened in the past... how many hours has it been since I talked to my mom?

"What day of the week is it?" I asked, hoping this wasn't one of those "passed out for days while I recovered" deals.

"Still Saturday. It's after noon, though it was nearly three in the morning when Carla got you here. Then you insisted that a dance party was in order. You danced and partied until you threw up in a plant and passed out on the floor. You've probably only been asleep about five hours." His fingers had moved from my face to my hand, thumb tracing circles along the ridge of my knuckles.

"Right, and *here* is?" I asked, squinting into the inky black darkness.

"R. B. Hayes Estate." He never let go of my hand, so I used it to gesture for him to keep going. "The location of last night's soiree."

"Why is it named after Rutherford B. Hayes?" I asked, wishing I hadn't drunk all the water.

Also that the water was coffee and in a much bigger cup...

Like a vat or maybe a keg... someone needed to invent a coffee keg.

"There are a number of safe estates in Ohio and they're all named after presidents who are from here." I felt him shrug.

"There are a number of? What is that number? Who came up with the phrase 'a number of'? Is that like something you say when you know there's more than one, but you didn't want to count? How many presidents could even be from Ohio?"

"Seven," he chuckled, and I gaped in the direction I thought he was.

"Seriously? This place birthed seven presidents? How and why? Also, why is it so damn dark?"

"First, yes, the second and third because that is what the electorate decided, but I don't think the state itself birthed them. If any of them or their mothers were alive, you'd probably be offered stretch marks proving they definitely slid out of a lady. It's dark because we are underground." He tugged me against his chest and then reached for something. A soft click, and the room filled with a warm light that was partially obscured by the man in front of me. After my eyes adjusted, I leaned away from

Cruz and noticed he was sporting a few stitches and a bruise on his cheek. His left arm was in a sling and there were dark circles under his eyes.

"Rough night, Stepford Soldier?" I asked, referencing my on-going insistence that he was really a robot. The man had never had so much as a hair out of place and he could turn attraction on and off like a light switch.

Seeing him look human bordered on disturbing.

"Everything was fine until I couldn't find you," his face betraying his normally stoic demeanor.

"Were you worried about me?" I mocked, fake punching his arm.

"Yes, Cyn," he spoke quietly and I felt my expression sober.

Instead of responding, I took a moment to look around the room. It was similar to a motel, with a double bed, a nightstand, a dresser with a TV on top and a desk with a chair. To the far left was an area that probably held the bathroom and sink portion, while against the wall by the door was a couch. It was like every La Quinta I'd ever stayed in, only instead of smelling like cleaner, it had a subtle lavender scent.

My eyes met Ian's and I knew he was waiting for me to acknowledge what he said. Except I didn't know how to deal with the concern and fear in his eyes, so I went with my old stand-by.

Complete verbal vomit.

"Sorry. I had the phone call open so you... or Carla... whoever I called could stay up to date. Then... I fell off the back of a van and it broke but might have survived if I hadn't accidentally dropped it in a parking lot and then it got run over by a truck. I'd have called you, but I didn't memorize your number, or Carla's..." my explanation cut off when he pressed his lips softly against mine in a gentle kiss.

"You did your job, I get it. But it's getting harder and harder to keep it together when you're in danger." He pressed his forehead against mine and Winnie scooted closer to place her head on my lap. "Winnie was also very concerned. Once she turned the unconscious Mr. Kade over to us, she panicked not being able to find you. Not sure I've ever seen her work so hard in her life."

I rubbed her ears and took a long breath.

"Sorry girl." My eyes went back to Cruz and I opened my mouth to say something, but it stuck in my throat. Instead I kissed him, hard and greedy until his lips parted and our tongues touched. His arms slipped around my torso and dragged the front of my body against him, devouring my lips as his hands roamed under my shirt.

Where he encountered one of my bruises and I flinched, letting out a squeak of pain.

He leaned back, breathing hard. My own respiratory rate was similarly afflicted and despite the sudden pain, I wanted more. My legs parted and I climbed into his lap, searching his eyes for some kind of permission.

"Are you sure?" He asked, voice breathy and I nodded.

"I'm tired of fighting, Ian," I whispered, crushing my mouth back against his. "Remind me there are things in this world that don't hurt."

Time had no meaning in Ian's arms. I lost track of the number of times he'd tortured me into bliss and he still wasn't tired.

"Stop! If you don't give me coffee, I'm committing murder," I shoved him off me and looked around for some clothes. "Also, I need food."

"I already ate, but I guess I could eat some more," he wiggled his eyebrows at me and I punched him in the arm.

"Seriously, you have to be a robot. No one has this much energy and charm without being battery powered," I grumbled, finding a shirt on the floor and pulling it on. I came across a pair of shorts and tugged those on too, struggling when they got to my thighs and hips.

I caught sight of my reflection in a window and verified that all the important bits were covered if not necessarily concealed. My bruises and scabs were on full display, but there was also nothing irritating the damaged skin.

Win win.

It was also apparent that these clothes belonged to Cruz and the only thing left on the floor were his jeans.

That's enough to cover his important bits, I decided and walked out of the room, Winnie on my heels.

Outside the room were a few dozen identical doors and hallways that branched off in both directions. At random, I headed to the left and continued to wonder at what this space was used for. The carpet was industrial and patterned to hide stains, similar to highly trafficked hotel areas. Every wall had crepe paper beige wall paper with floral patterns in a neutral and un-stimulating shade.

The end of the hallway had a fire door that led to a staircase and I started up the concrete steps. Every sound and step was amplified and I reached down to stroke Winnie as my heart rate started climbing.

What if we were all captured and this is the stairway to the big bad boss who wants information? I looked to Winnie for signs of concern, but her fur remained unruffled. *Bowser probably wasn't alarming to the dog, since he was a winged turtle but those fire shells were no joke.*

We kept going up until the staircase ended at another fire door with a crash bar but no window. I pressed my face against the door, listening for signs of life on the other side but the metal was too thick.

"You got my back?" I whispered to Winnie and she wagged her tail. "On three then."

I held up my index finger, then middle and finally thumb, storming through the metal door into...

"A pantry?" I asked, looking down at her. I traced my finger along the shelves and found spices, cans and bags of flour. "It is a pantry."

To the left, a sliver of light came in from the floor. Winnie and I inched closer, and I pressed my head to the wall to listen.

The wall gave, swinging outward and dropping me to the floor.

"Fu-" I started, Winnie jumping on my back and out into the room. Her collar jingled in what I interpreted as a prance, and I braved lifting my face a few inches from the floor.

I was on tile, looking at the bottom of wooden cabinets. Probably it was a kitchen, so I raised my head a little higher and nearly dropped it again in horror.

Half the kitchen was completely decimated.

If I hadn't seen the kitchen yesterday, I would think it was in the middle of a remodel. Most of the prep counters were scorched, or no longer standing. The fridge had dents shaped like bullets and possibly a human head. Scarred black patches graced the once white cabinetry and the oven was no more.

"What the hell happened?" I whispered, hauling myself to my feet and looking through the open doorway to the rest of the house. "What caused..."

I choked out a sob when I saw the far counter.

Sitting in shattered ruins of melted plastic and petrified glass, was the coffee maker.

"No! Why?" I ran over, trying to see if any part of it was salvageable or capable of giving me the elixir of the gods. "What kind of monster would do this to you? Tell me, please?"

Tears streamed down my face and Winnie sat on my foot, offering her head as comfort.

"If you're done having a meltdown, coffee is out here," Carla's voice floated from somewhere in the ether surrounding the Earth. "Also, whose underwear are you wearing?"

Determining the voice was as real as the bounding ache in my skull, I turned around and followed her into the dining room. While the kitchen looked like the remnants of a war zone, the next room over was as pristine and intact as it had been the night before aside from a few dark patches on the shared kitchen wall and a liquid spot on the carpet.

Four people were seated around the table, all wearing more than underwear. Since I had a dog, I decided that my clothing choices were above reproach. My eyes swept the neighboring rooms to see that they were clean, orderly and not sporting signs of a fiery explosion.

Only the kitchen had been obliterated, but I had still slept underground.

"Oh, thank dog," I said, walking over to the carafe and grabbing a dish. I filled it with coffee, added a bit of honey and gulped. My tongue and throat were scorched, but every sip was worth the pain when some of the fog I was feeling faded.

"Did you just use a bowl as a coffee mug?" I turned to the man who entered, Conri Kade in jeans and a T-shirt, looking more normal than he had in the linen garb last night.

"This is a coffee mug," I said, lifting it to my lips by the rim and trying to drink without dumping it down the front of my stolen shirt or burning the tips of my fingers.

"It is not, there is no handle," he gestures to the opposite of the coffee machine. "Those are coffee mugs."

It was a small, generic, probably ten-ounce cup and I scoffed at him.

"Handles don't mean anything. In Chinese restaurants, the teacups for the jasmine green tea don't have handles," I countered, slugging back more.

"But this is not tea, it is coffee. And coffee mugs have handles," he gestured again at the pathetic beverage containers.

"That is not a coffee mug. It's a shot glass and I don't have the patience necessary to drink coffee in those quantities. What happened to the kitchen?" I polished off my coffee bowl and poured another. Everyone watched as I crossed the room and chose a seat, sliding into the dining room chair near Carla.

She was in a suit with a pink button-down. Beside her another man I recognized from last night's security detail, Joel. Across from Joel was the person I'd met at Mr. Kade's regular residence who went over the binders and general strategy for last night's disaster.

Or... detail. Depending on which side of the event we were on.

"It became an epicenter, and we found at least one person who had snuck in under the guise of a friend while being foe. The explosive you found, though removed, made the area one of interest and was heavily monitored. A lot of the indoor incidents happened there," the man from Mr. Kade's house supplied and I looked at him, assessing the tan slacks and salmon colored-polo with his weasel shaped face. His name was Alec or Alan... maybe Glen?

"You look weird and kind of suspicious. Did you do it?" I asked, using my thumb and index finger to drink my coffee bowl.

"Ms. Sharp, that's insulting!" He blustered and I couldn't tell if it was guilt or entitled white man feelings throwing him off. "You can't just go around flinging accusations like monkey feces at the zoo!"

"Winnie, check," I said, and she popped up from keeping my bare feet warm. With a jingling prance, she approached Alec/Alan/Glen and while he was still giving me a stink eye, shoved her nose in his crotch and took a series of four short sniffs.

He screamed, and Winnie pranced back to flop on my feet.

"What did you determine, Ms. Sharp?" Mr. Kade asked with a smile on his face and I shrugged before draining my coffee bowl.

"That he is startled by having a dog nose shoved in his junk."

Cruz walked in, bypassing the coffee pot to slide gracefully into the seat next to me, leaning in to press a kiss on my temple. My face warmed and I wished my coffee mug wasn't empty.

"You're a robot. An inhuman, inhumane, robotic syntho-" I stopped talking to drink more coffee, then sighed loudly when it was still empty. The man had just made my body come alive in new and surprising ways despite the fact that it was mostly a scabby bruise. I could forgive him for his un-caffeinated existence.

Also his shoulder sling got lost during our morning shenanigans and I was a little worried about his arm.

"At any rate," Carla began and all eyes turned to her. "We need to debrief Cyn and come up with a plan. Last night was a cluster and if we can't get a handle on the incident, we'll blow Mr. Kade's cover and we'll have even more people to worry about."

"Didn't Cruz debrief me last night?" I furrowed my brow, trying to remember anything after the conversation with my mom, but I polished off the open bottle of tequila after finishing the whiskey at the request of the bartender and it was all a bit fuzzy. However I came to be here when Cruz "debriefed" me this morning was as vague and mysterious as the basis of this entire operation.

"You were too drunk to debrief last night, so we had to bring you here to ensure you spoke to us before anyone else." Weasel

Man's voice was as grating as his personality and I felt extremely uncomfortable with the way he said "debrief".

Almost like he had wanted to do last night what Cruz did this morning and I stopped him. If that were true, then I was going to need to start wearing a body cam and electrocution underwear.

Probably zappy protection panties existed.

Just wouldn't want to get them wet.

"I fell off a moving vehicle! I deserved to be drunk and my briefs are mine to wear!" I snapped at him. "Also, I had to ask my mom personal questions. Very detailed and personal questions and I didn't want to remember the answers and those are the only things I know with absolute clarity!"

It was as close to sharing as I was prepared to be. People who didn't already know about my mom deserved the bliss of ignorance. Those who did could infer enough to not ask any follow-up questions.

"Yes, that does look painful. If you'd like to rest, I'd be happy to debrief you in private," Mr. Kade said with a wink and my face burned. A sound similar to a snarl came out of Cruz and Mr. Kade gave a little too knowing of a chuckle. "I believe I know whose underwear she's wearing, Carla. You owe me ten dollars."

My sister in law bored a hole into the side of my head with her eyes as she slapped a bill on the table. In the interest of self-preservation, I continued to stare at my coffee bowl and trace the rim. I tried to will coffee from the carafe across the table into it, but succeeded only in giving myself a headache.

Telekinesis, like good decision making, continued to elude me.

Stuck at the center of attention, I tried to get back on topic.

"So, last night Winnie and I were watching Mr. Kade and Cruz came over to allow me a break. We took a step outside and I saw movement on the tree line. As we approached, we discovered a small number of masked men. They attacked, we fought back, and ultimately Winnie successfully took a bite out of crime."

Everyone returned to business faces and I breathed out a sigh of relief.

"Did you recognize any of the attackers?" Joel asked, and he retrieved a spiral bound notebook from beside him.

"Yes, the first man Winnie and I attacked together, I believe he was Femi from the binders," I stopped when the whole table went completely silent. "What?"

"How sure are you?" Carla asked and I noticed Conri wringing his fingers.

"Very sure. When I removed the mask, he had a scar over his left eye the size of a fingernail and the dimple in his chin. It would be impossible not to recognize him. Only... I can't remember which binder he was in." I studied Weasel Man, knowing he would give the most away.

I was right, Femi was supposed to be in the "good guys" binder.

"So... What does this all mean? Where are we going from here?" Everyone looked to each other for the answer to my question. "Were you able to do anything with the blue van's remnants? It didn't have a license plate, but was there anything useful inside?"

Everyone shifted again and Cruz leaned in to whisper in my ear.

"All of that information is classified, and no one is allowed to tell you."

"Interesting. I can risk my life for people but I can't know why. How fluffing delightful. So, I guess we're all done, then?" I asked moving to stand up. As much as information would have been nice, I had other things to do then sit in the dark while everyone else got flashlights.

Like finding my missing Canadians and converting everything Cruz did to long term memory. When he left, I was going to need those memories.

"I need to head home."

"I'll take you," Carla answered, and I nodded. I offered a hand to Joel and one to Mr. Kade.

"It was nice working with you both. Hopefully this gets sorted out," I said and Conri shook his head.

"This isn't goodbye, Ms. Sharp. Your services are still required and we will be in touch."

I shrugged and looked at the other man at the table. Weasel Man was looking offended that I hadn't offered him a hand and I considered making it right, but his hands looked gross.

Soft and clammy, like they'd never done any proper work in their life.

"If you need my help again, you'll need to help me with information. I'm not going in blind. Either I get the full picture, or you find another canine," my eyes landed on Joel and he chewed his cheek before offering me a single jerk of his head in agreement.

"Great. My suit is toast, so I'm definitely ready to go home when you are."

Carla finished her drink and looked me over, considering my borrowed outfit.

"Probably I should find you some different clothes before we go. If you wear that, I'll have to answer far too many questions." She led me from the room and back to the kitchen pantry. "I realize these rooms are secured for a reason but why are the only entry and exit points the secret ones? The other one is in the back of a coat closet."

"What? I can wear someone else's underwear home. It's not a big deal, I live alone except for Winnie and she's seen it," I complained, but continued following her. She entered one of the generic doors and I saw a duffle on the bed. She reached in and pulled out leggings and a top.

"I bring clothes everywhere, carry over from years of never knowing where I'll wake up. We don't have time to go to your apartment," she said while I tossed off Cruz's clothes and put on hers. I wasn't the least endowed woman, but I was grateful Carla had left me in the dust when it came to breasts. I didn't need a bra to wear her shirt, though it was a crop top with our height difference and the leggings were capris. Her gratuitous hips made sure the pants accommodated my stomach and ass, so the trade off was worth it. "I'm supposed to deliver you directly to your mother."

"What? Why?" I choked on my own spit. As mysterious as her clothing bag was, being handed over to my mother was far more insulting than not being given a heads up.

"Because apparently you called her last night with questions regarding seniors porn in the area and you agreed to attend a screening party in exchange for her calling me to pick you up." She checked her watch and tossed me some socks. "And we're already late."

Chapter Thirteen:
Leaning Toward
Mean

"**I** will give you all the coffee in my apartment, as well as my Jeep if you pretend you forgot and take me home," I begged Carla as she pulled the SUV from last night to the curb. "I'd run there myself but I don't have shoes."

The front lawn of my childhood home looked like the queue for Rocky Horror Picture Show. People were wearing boxers, garters and nightgowns, most of them old enough to have seen it in the movie in theaters on its original release date.

Legally drunk and with offspring.

The town was probably completely without gold spandex and fishnets after this group got done.

It was an omen for what to expect inside and I was against it.

"All the coffee in your apartment is more than Seth and I can drink in a year," she scoffed and I wiggled my eyebrows.

"You'll have more energy for *other* things?" I followed it with a *bom chicka wow wow.*

"I'll get you out of this if you tell me why you were wearing Cruz's underwear when I put you to bed in your own underwear and there were no other clothes in the room?"

I chewed on my bottom lip, looking between her and the people on my parent's lawn. While visually the group in front of me were more offensive than the proposed topic, emotionally the ramifications of admitting what I did were more than I could handle at the moment.

If ever.

If I never talked about it, I never needed to acknowledge if I felt good or bad about my decisions.

Though feeling good was definitely a factor on which Cruz had physically delivered.

Mentally I was on the fence.

"Fine," I grumbled, pushing open my door and putting my sock covered feet on the sidewalk.

"Seriously?" She grabbed my hand and I tilted my head toward her as I popped open the back door for Winnie. "You'd rather witness whatever is happening in there then tell me what happened this morning?"

"Yup. Because I know that *that* has a time limit," I jerked my thumb toward the house. "This conversation could have never-ending judgment, consequences, and emotional baggage I'm not ready to acknowledge... possibly ever."

Carla scrunched her face in thought and I tugged my wrist out of her hand. Winnie was sitting beside me and I rubbed her head, shutting the back door.

"Can I ask one question?" Carla asked, as I went to close the passenger side door.

"You can, but whether or not I answer it..." I shrugged and she nodded. Chewing on her bottom lip, she thought carefully for a minute before blowing out a breath and looking me in the eyes.

"Do you know what you're doing with all of this?"

I swallowed and looked at my feet.

"Not a clue," I answered, shutting the door. She rolled down the window and I raised a brow.

"I only agreed to one question, do you have another?"

Carla smirked and shook her head.

"Nah, I just wanted to let you know that your mom bought you a costume and you would have been better off keeping Cruz's underwear because now you're going to be Magenta," she cackled, and pulled away from the curb.

"What?" I looked down at Winnie and she was smiling, her tongue hanging to the side. "If I'm Magenta, you're totally Columbia."

She let out a loud fart and wagged her foul stench into the air.

"I'm taking that as consent. You have to wear the hat," I told her and we started toward the front door before my mother stepped out dressed like...

"Oh my dog…" I whispered, taking in her shimmering gold bathing suit bottom over sheer panty hose and what may have been pasties over her otherwise exposed chest. "She's the creature of the night."

"Cynthia! You're late!" She called to me and I tried to cover Winnie's innocent eyes. The dog may have stuffed her nose in many people's private areas and witnessed Larry and I hooking up… also now Cruz, but she didn't need this mental image. "Get in here!"

"We played with fire and we got burned, girl," I whispered, walking past the line of costumed seniors. "Still better than talking about our feelings."

Six hours later, I was standing in my apartment.

Night had fallen and any of the remaining mental stability I possessed fell beside it.

"There were just so many…" I whispered, staring at my couch. "It was like erotic fan fiction on film and no one knew where to point the camera."

We'd been in the room for five minutes, and I couldn't move. Winnie had gotten water, shoved her food dish into my leg, and flopped on the ground beside the coffee table. Every few seconds, her eyebrows would wiggle toward me and she'd let out an unhappy grumble.

"How can you consider eating after what we've witnessed? Especially *Cloudy with a Chance of Man Juice*?" She looked indifferent and I forced my feet forward, wincing at the pinch of heels. "I mean, making Rocky Horror into a porn makes sense.

It wasn't for me, but who pervs up an animated movie about feeding the world?"

I slid off the pointy toed monstrosities beside the couch and padded to the kitchen in my nylons.

"Shiitake Mushrooms!" I screamed, my foot slipping in Winnie's water spill and sending me to the floor of the kitchen on my slutty maid clad ass. I laid in the puddle, waiting for the glitter rain I caused to settle onto the floor where it will remain forevermore.

Both because glitter is the herpes of crafts and because I had no interest in standing up.

Winnie shoved her face against mine, licking every inch she could connect with under my teased and sprayed hair. While I would have gone the wig route for Magenta's hair, my mom insisted that styling my real hair was the only way to go.

The bruises and curling iron burns would haunt me for weeks of showers to come.

"You're lucky you're cute, kid," I grumbled, crawling to her food storage cabinet. "Because you're an ass."

She didn't disagree, ramming her food bowl into my ribs.

"Such an ass," I muttered again, grabbing the scoop and dumping some crunchies into her bowl.

My apron started shaking and after a moment of panic, I discovered it had a pocket that was holding yet another new cell phone Carla had stopped for me to acquire on the way home.

"Hello?" I said, not sure who the caller was with my complete list of contacts obliterated along with my phone in a parking lot.

"Cyn," Larry's husky voice filled the line and my heart hammered in my chest.

"Yeah?" I breathed into the line, my scalp tingling as moisture spilled from my arm pits and under boob.

"Are you home? Alone?" He asked and I looked around. "No?"

"Are you asking me or telling me?" His response pulled me out of my fog.

"Telling. I'm home but Winnie is here, so I'm technically not alone." I held back my thoughts before they could escape. I might miss him, but I wasn't going back to him either.

Not after *her*.

More, not until his mom stopped acting like I was something she stepped on in a pasture.

He sighed loudly and I could hear hands scrubbing his face with calloused palms.

"I'm not... this is awkward, but I need to ask you about today."

"We're broken up, Larry. I can have sex with whoever I want, and you don't get to ask questions. Not after your Suzy's Diner date with Amber!" I snapped at him, but the line was eerily silent. "Are you there? Did you hear me?"

"You slept with someone else?" It was nearly an inaudible whisper.

"Yes," I barked, but bile rose in my throat. Not only was admitting this hard, the pain radiating through his end of the phone was worse. Part of me wanted him to hurt, to know how it felt to feel meaningless to someone you care about.

The other part of me felt like an asshole, but I elected to ignore her and continue digging my emotional hole.

"Are you happy now? You know about today."

"It... it was today?" He stammered and I blinked back at the phone.

"Yeah... isn't that what you called about?"

"No. I called about today's... screening," he clarified, and I nodded down at Winnie who was scarfing her food like it was the last in the universe and I was a neglectful dog mom.

"Oh... that was disturbing. What do you want to know about it?" I asked, stroking Winnie's fur and wondering if I should apologize for my confession.

"In any of the movies... I'm sorry, who did you have sex with?" He'd moved on from sad to pissed off and I flinched slightly.

"Use your telephone voice, man! It took a lot of alcohol to make it through this event. My mom made me dress as Magenta and that meant heels. Wicked, pointy, work of the devil footwear that makes no sense for someone my height unless they are a drag queen," I rubbed my temples and pretended to be drunk even though he couldn't see me.

There had been no desire for alcohol after last night's foray into the land of ethanol. While I might be mildly irresponsible, I was too old to get that wasted twice in one month.

Larry, however, was better off not knowing that I was sober so I could blame the alcohol if I got annoyed and hung up on him.

"Who did you have sex with?" He shouted again and I held the phone two feet from my face.

"Stop yelling. It's none of your business. What's your question?" I nearly shouted back over the line and I was surprised his anger didn't melt the phone in my hand over the line.

"Who did you have sex with?"

"Besides that!"

He took a few deep breaths that I assume were intended to keep him from having a stroke.

"Did any of the men in the movie have a Mighty Ducks logo tattooed on his left butt cheek?" His words were clipped, factual.

"Yeah. I think in... *Ferris Bueller's Jerk-Off*, why?" I asked, not mentioning that the tattoo and its owner had been two of the more exciting portions of that flick. The scene with the principal and Mr. Bueller's "legal guardian", a grandma-esque figure who seduced the faux principal into losing track of her charge with her 'appetizing apples'.

Ferris had to pay for "muffins" from a shop with a serenade and a lollipop.

The lollipop being a portion of his anatomy that held zero resemblance to candy.

"I just got an email from my cousin in Canada. Her brother was headed down here to look for work and went missing after he crossed the border. Cody wasn't exactly playing with a full deck, but being a muscle-bound meathead, she didn't worry anyone would hurt him. Mostly she worried someone had traded him magic beans for his life's savings. Yesterday, she got a hastily scrawled postcard stamped from this area saying he can't believe everyone in porn is just an immigrant working off their debt to

America. That this country is a real blessing for men with 'big dicks and limited skills'. An insult to his co-star if you ask me."

"Their... debt to America? With their penises? What the heck? Did she send you a picture of the postcard? Does she live in this area?" I asked, climbing to my feet and pulling out a jug of cold brew. I drank heavily from the container, not minding that it was only subtly vanilla scented.

"Yeah, I'll send you the picture. But that's the weird part. She lives in upstate New York. He could have traveled to the neighboring province and dropped down, but the agency she worked with insisted he needed to immigrate in through Saskatchewan." I worried my lip as I listened, wondering what the odds were that I'd seen all my missing men today on film in the nude.

On film, in the buff, giving it to a lady older than my parents by at least a decade.

"Did she have any info on the people or persons she worked with to coordinate his immigration?" I was scrunching my face in thought, but I hadn't been focused on anything above the belt line in the movies.

Human instinct said to look, and I definitely looked.

Gravity did not go easy on women.

"Yeah, Ruth. A mobility-limited older woman who lived near Sweet Pea."

"Let me guess, all traces of her have suddenly and miraculously disappeared?" I put the coffee jug back in the fridge and trudged to my bed, landing on it face first.

"I'm guessing there are more?" He asked and I nodded into my pillow.

"At least two. All muscle-bound Canadians with limited educational background and significant experience with their hands and things which impale," I sighed, wishing this story were national news so men can feel fear and terror like every woman does.

Probably half would just ask where the auditions were and how much it paid.

"Was it one of those two you had sex with?" He demanded again and I let out a sigh.

"Did you not hear me? They're missing! If I knew where they were to have sex with them, I wouldn't have said they were missing! Besides, if you didn't want me to have sex with someone else, you shouldn't have groped and let a mostly naked Amber ride you. You should have stood up to your mom and told her that I was important to you. But this is where we are, Larry. So who and what I do doesn't concern you. Send me the damn picture."

"It matters because if it's anyone I know, I'm going to kill them," he snarled, and I banged my head into my pillow. "No one I know should be touching you. You're mine, Cyn!"

"You're an idiot," I muttered into the phone and ended the call, waiting for him to send the picture.

Chapter Fourteen: Flirting with Fire

I spent the next morning sifting through documents.

Mr. Johnson's files were the most organized and Larry's sister's the least. Sitting in the middle was Noah's sister, Robin, whose files bordered on the sociopathic. She had kept everything and added her own notes to each item in a script that I anticipated one day seeing in a museum exhibit about terrorists.

While that sounds like a gift, the gum wrapper she scribbled on when she couldn't find a piece of paper to draw the number 2 was not enlightening.

She also could not remember what it meant or why it was important.

None of the documents were unique. I could print identical contracts with slightly varied language from the Internet. The women they worked with had used numbers that must have belonged to burner phones as well as URLs that were both easy to find and generic enough to make tracing them nearly impossible with bot registration and sales.

"What is all that?" Stella asked, startling me out of my trance.

"Immigration scam... maybe human trafficking," I sighed and looked over my part time intern who would be returning to college in just under a month. Stella had long straight hair, a literal relationship to all words, and an affinity for mystery that would have made her a card-carrying member of the Mystery Machine Club in the 70's.

We'd met a few months ago sitting on a bench. She also sold a toy house as a real house by accident, helped rescue me from walking home in extreme heat, and taught me more than I wanted to know about high school drama.

"Like Lizandro or different?" She asked, referencing the farmer who was threatened with deportation for not getting all the rubber stamps needed to make the government happy.

"Different. Someone helped them immigrate and then... took them. But the weird part is that at least one of them was featured in a porn festival my mom forced me to sit through. Possibly all of them."

"Why only possibly? Have you watched these films?" She tilted her head slightly and rubbed Winnie's ears. The dog had practically knocked the young woman over when she walked in and I would have been jealous if I had the energy.

As it was, I only had coffee.

"I only have face pictures and I wasn't watching the faces," I shrugged. "I'll have to re-watch them but I'm not really motivated to ask my mom for copies."

"Would you like me to watch them? Maybe James can help. He's good with details." I cackled at her simple statement. "What did I say?"

"You said you wanted to watch porn with your boyfriend and that you would do it as a favor to me," I cackled again and the bell on the front door jingled as another person walked in, but I kept my focus on Stella.

"Is it not normal to watch porn with one's boyfriend?" She asked and the man who entered choked, forcing us both to turn and look at him. "Or is it just not normal to do it casually?"

"Can we help you?" I asked him, noting his pink tinged ears.

"M-m-maybe," he stuttered and I tilted my head. "I h-h-heard you can h-h-help with problems."

He swallowed hard and I blinked at his wringing hands. The man was probably in his forties with thinning hair and crow's feet beside eyes that were a faded brown. Like his whole face had suffered at the hands of the sun and he hadn't bothered with a fresh coat of paint.

"What kind of problems? And did you use the plural because you have more than one or did you use it because that is how Cyn was represented to you?" Stella asked in her usual tone of clipped curiosity. Her ability to make details people would overlook whole lines of inquiry was one of my favorite things about working with her.

"B-both. It's a-about a g-girl." His pink ears went scarlet at his declaration.

"Dude, I'm not a love doctor or a drug dealer," I said, crossing my arms and trying to decide when I could safely run away.

"N-n-no. I don't n-need her to l-love me. I n-need her to h-have s-s-sex. A m-m-male and a f-f-female mating." His stutter made me both impatient and terrified that the word following the repeated syllable would be more horrible than the one before.

"Are these animals or people?" Stella asked and I was immediately grateful for her literal mind.

"P-p-people," he said.

"Welp, I can't help with that. If they don't want to do it, you can't get them to do it," I shrugged but he just shook his head.

"N-n-no. They w-want to. It's just... we have b-b-bad luck. F-first the chickens... t-then it w-was the power outage... W-worst was the f-f-fires." A bead of sweat traveled down the side of his face, taking the ravine of fine lines to his chin before splashing on his flannel shirt.

"So... what do you want from me?" I asked, checking Stella's expression to see if she'd figured it out first.

We were both clueless.

"I-if you stood out-out-side, you could draw the disaster to you and w-we could finally..."

"Oh my dog. Are you saying you need a disaster magnet to guard your house while you do the nasty?" My face flamed red at the implications. I was so well known for causing chaos, people were soliciting me for disaster services. I was this close to needing a website so I could charge to perform at parties and hold seances.

"Most of those disasters were only peripherally my fault. It's not like me standing outside your house would somehow prevent them from getting inside. There's also no guarantee that if a disaster came at me it would stop with me. Your house could become an epicenter with me outside it."

"Outside the b-b-bedroom door," he clarified, and I started to hyperventilate.

"You want me to listen?" I gasped, torn between tears and laughter at the insanity of existence.

"N-n-o... Unless you hear s-s-something n-not right. Then if you c-could help?" His face was now a shade beneath eggplant on the color wheel and I pinched my arm to check if this was real. "P-p-please? It's im-important."

Stella nodded with understanding.

"Would you like me to sit outside his bedroom or watch the pornography films in your mother's possession?" Stella asked and I gaped at her. Her expression was innocent and declared if the man felt it was important enough to ask for it, it was important enough for us to do.

Technically, he would be the one to *do it*.

We were being asked to stand guard and listen like voyeurs.

I banged my head several times on the desk muttering *why me*.

"You both know that neither of these things are normal, right?" I lifted my head and my gaze went back and forth between the two of them but neither backed down from their request. "Fine, whatever."

I handed Stella the pictures of my Canadians.

"These are the men you are looking for. I don't have any naked pictures, so you're going to have to do what you can to watch their faces and ID them. Fair warning, their faces are rarely in focus in the film."

"I'll be certain to watch carefully and re-watch until I'm certain," Stella promised and I shook my head.

"Yeah, sure. Good luck, I guess. Tell James what you're making him watch, and why, before you invite him so he can get the laughter out before the screening."

I rolled my eyes at her solemn nod when she started texting on her cell. My gaze went to the man standing there.

"What's your name?"

"Ch-ch-Charlie," he said and I nodded, motioning for him to lead the way out of my office.

"Nice to meet you Charlie. The second I hear either your or your lady friend orgasm, I am out."

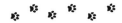

Charlie lived in a two-story farmhouse halfway between the dairy and Sweet Pea's "downtown" area. While he had offered to drive me to his house, I elected to have my own vehicle for immediate departure when no tornados, electrical storms or ancient Incan idols came to life and foiled their fornication plans.

Apparently, they had been trying to consummate their marriage for nearly six months and I was the only contributing factor to their failed coital success post nuptials. It was not that they *hadn't* had sex, Charlie was quick-ish to clarify, just not since they had been married a few months after I returned home.

I was also assured neither of them was a screamer, a fact that would haunt me until I die when he turned out to be a liar. Both he and his wife had screamed deity praises so loud, I'd have thought a televangelist was giving a sermon.

One that was designed for dogs and children if the howling was any indication.

"Why me?" I asked Winnie in the rearview mirror. She had wisely stayed in the car, AC blasting, while I had listened at the door while strangers got down and dirty in their marital bed. There had been no threats to their privacy aside from a stray bee and a motor vehicle accident where a car horn got stuck in the on position.

None of these things had stopped the copulating couple from reaching nirvana.

Loudly, and with great praise to the holy spirit.

"I need a shower."

Dropping the car into reverse, I backed out and drove toward the main highway. At the stop sign, I looked left and then right, feeling inclined to turn left and drive toward the dairy. A few days had passed since I was there and I needed visual confirmation that it had survived in my absence. It was Sunday, making me reasonably sure Joseph wouldn't be there to yell at me, so I made the turn.

"If anything is having sex there, though, I'm breaking my own rules and getting wasted for a second time this month," I informed my partner. She responded with a foghorn snore and pawed at the air.

"I'm going to take that as an agreement," I told her, continuing down the highway toward the dairy. It was mid-afternoon and the parking lot was half-filled with minivans covered in stick families. The ice cream line was out the door and loud, small humans racing through the dirt parking lot waving fingers coated in multi-colored goo that probably had once been ice cream. My Jeep rolled past the driveway and to the dirt lot on the far side of the pasture where employees park.

There were only two cars present, both belonging to farm hands that handled weekend feedings. We all took turns coming in on the weekends, including me though I wasn't allowed to feed the animals after I tried to feed them to each other.

I pulled beside a faded white pick-up truck and put the Jeep in park, looking out at the pastures and fenced-off paddocks.

Relaxed, I got out and stretched my arms overhead. Several vertebrae popped and I looked back at my sleeping partner.

"Are you coming?"

She rolled over and I checked the dashboard temperature.

"Yeah, ninety-five is a bit much," I muttered, leaving the engine on and shutting the doors. There was no point in locking it. Beyond not having an extra key, I really didn't think anyone would keep the car once Winnie's chemical warfare kicked in.

The dog could clear out a Best Buy on Black Friday.

My feet carried me toward the red barn and I paused to pet a donkey who put her head in my path. I took comfort in the fact that she wanted my affection. Despite not being permitted at work these past few days, it didn't look like anyone, or anything, had missed a beat in my absence.

"Nothing like an unbothered farm to remind me I'm not that important to this place, either," I whispered to Ethel, thinking that Larry, the farm and the Army were better off without me. "At least you like me."

The donkey heehawed and trotted off.

"Right. Only in small doses." I grumbled, walking toward the barn and considering checking the output stores just to be sure the area wouldn't run out of ice cream or cheese.

At the rate I was going through both, it was a true civic duty.

Rounding the corner, a voice carried over the hum of the high-powered fan.

"We didn't have a choice. There was no way to get past the security. He knew we were coming." The man nearly shouted and I paused in the doorway to listen. "I told you, demanding he appear in person was a dead giveaway. We would have been better off waiting for him to make a move than showing our hand."

My heartrate kicked up and I tried to calm my breathing to hear better as I crept closer to a stall. They were near the open-air arena, a place to trot livestock for sale and birth calves without everyone feeling claustrophobic and getting covered in after-birth. If the echo provided sonographic assistance, they were on the side of the farm closer to the steer, opposite where the employee parking lot and the ice cream shop sat.

"We lost six men, including Femi. He was our inside line, what are we left with? He needs to be exposed if we want to live a normal life." A second man spoke, his heavily accented English reminded me that if these men were trying to get to Conri Kade, he had enemies the world over. While Russia was a difficult ally to imagine, the possibility was there.

"We still have that American," the first man spoke again and I leaned in closer. "He is stupid, but not without his merits. He'd trade anything to keep his money-making scheme under wraps."

"I don't think he can get us another shot, not without blowing his cover. All of C.K.'s contacts are under scrutiny. They may have replaced the whole team with American soldiers at this point," the second man spoke before punching something that cracked beneath his knuckles. "Why would they work so hard to protect him?"

"What do you mean 'why'? The Americans brought him here, why wouldn't they protect him? Without a scapegoat, the public could learn the truth."

I slipped around the corner to see a blonde man in cargos and a T-shirt, standing with hands on hips. Facing him was a man whose knuckles were dripping blood, a cigarette bobbing in the corner of his mouth beneath jet-black hair in white chocolate skin.

"But why? You know they were in on the attack. The weapons were..." The screech of instrumental country music broke through the barn, and I froze, feeling my pants shake with the ringtone.

"It's her!" The blonde-haired man shouted and I grabbed the phone from my pocket when the second man produced a black semi-automatic. "Keep an eye out for the dog!"

A shot rang out and I dropped to the ground, throwing my phone at the shooter. Sparks accompanied the sound of shattered glass as it intersected his bullet. The music stopped and I low-crawled through the shaved wood until I reached the corner and stumbled upright before running flat out toward the Jeep.

"Get her!" One of the men shouted and I pumped my legs faster, diving in between the wooden cross beams of an animal enclosure and landing face first in a muddy puddle. Panicked, I wiggled deeper until I was completely covered in the muck.

"Where did she go?" One of the men shouted, and I held my breath against the smell of manure mixed with urine as a creature bleated above me.

My eyes were too caked in mud to see the men, and I took shallow breaths trying to listen for footsteps or gunfire.

"Shit! Go that way, I'll check over there!" It sounded like the man with black hair was giving orders and I heard the heavy tread of a man toward the dairy. A softer voice cooed toward the sheep above me.

"It would be a privilege to end her and her dog, wouldn't it?" The sheep above me bleated again and he fired twice on the animal, sending it to the ground with a heavy thud beside me. "Death at my gun is a blessing. You won't want to see what we have planned for her, little one."

Chapter Fifteen:
Walk of Blame

"**Y**ou need to fill me in, completely," I told Cruz as we stood in front of my building. Mud dripped from the tip of my nose to mingle with the clumps falling from everywhere else. Despite the drive from the farm to downtown, the mud hadn't crusted and the blood of Sheldon the sheep was still fresh. The interior of my Jeep was a nightmare for both hemophobes and rhypophobes alike. "Who the hell is Conri?"

He stood with one hand on his hips, the other held to his chest. We should probably have tried harder to find his sling, but the doctor only wanted him to wear it for a day. Every expression he could have shared was kept guarded with a mask of indifference and a general passivity to the world as a whole. His muscular body was clean and flawless in a plain black shirt and jeans, but

I could see the wheels turning behind his eyes. No matter how much lust or concern he conveyed, the man was all business underneath and there was a very real possibility that being with me was just a convenient detour on an ongoing assignment.

Like those sailors with a woman at every port.

Whatever he'd planned when I found him standing outside my apartment was long gone from his mind.

"Are you covered in blood?" He asked, studying the various drips coming off of me.

"Answer my question first, Cruz! Or I swear on my mother's sex toy collection that I will castrate you and sell your testicles as Rocky Mountain oysters to the highest bidder. What the hell did you and Carla pull me into?" His eyes danced with amusement at my threat, so I threw a roundhouse kick at his ribs.

He dodged it, barely, but his face sobered.

"Call Carla, there are things she knows that I don't," he said softly and I shook my head, flinging mud everywhere.

"I can't call her. A madman shot my cell phone," I huffed, turning away from him to the wooden door that led to my office. It took three tries to get my muddy fingers to guide the key into the lock, but once I released the bolt, I stumbled through the door and shouted for Winnie.

"Get your ass in here, you fluffy chicken."

Ears flat, tail between her legs, she slunk past me in disgrace. The scent of blood when I got in the car had alarmed her. When my fear turned to anger at the sight of Ian Cruz in front of my office building, she'd begun to whimper.

"Cyn," Cruz began, but I shot him a death glare.

"Call Carla, I'm taking a shower and then you jerks are giving me answers."

He nodded without comment, taking out his phone and working the keys. Satisfied he was following instructions, I moved toward the door in the rear of my office. It was still locked, and I released the bolt before climbing the stairs and stripping in front of the door to my bathroom.

None of my clothes could be saved.

"Carla is on her way," Cruz said as his feet came to a stop at the landing to my apartment. "Do you..."

His throat constricted, cutting off sound when I looked at him.

"You... aren't wearing clothes," his voice was strangled and my eyes narrowed at him.

"True, but I'm wearing blood and mud. You want to contribute to the mess? You don't have mud but I can draw your blood." I countered, and he took a step closer. Followed by another before his hand found my waist and he gave a gentle squeeze.

"I have something else I can cover you with," he whispered, moving his lips closer to the soft spot just below my ear and I shuddered. "It isn't blood, but I make it myself."

My lady parts clenched and I fought my lungs to take in air.

"What's in it for me?" My voice came out breathy and I wanted to hit myself for giving into the effect he had on me. The man was a machine, he could turn on and off the charm as easily as a go-cart on a track.

"There are a few things we didn't do the other night... want to try them now?" His mouth had moved to mine while his fingers slid up to my breasts. "I can promise by the end of the shower you'll be clean, satisfied and no longer tense."

"Uhn..." was all I got out before his mouth crashed against mine and he backed me into the bathroom.

Body clean, mind calm-ish and core throbbing, I stumbled into the kitchen to start a pot of coffee. Cruz had taken the edge of panic off my anger and now I knew that my anger was not only justified, but an excellent motivator to bruise the parts of Cruz I could get my teeth on. Now that I had put on sweatpants and a baggy T-shirt, my flesh was covered but I still felt naked. My wet hair stuck to my neck while Cruz reclined on the couch, eyeing me like a cat who ate the canary.

Ironic, considering in this instance, I was the cat but he'd still done the eating.

"Are you feeling better, chica?" He asked, and I didn't miss the smug smirk on his lips. His hair was damp, but there was no other indicator that he'd just been in the shower with me. Proving that no matter how quickly he could turn on and off the charm, he was dangerous when wet.

Well, wet and now commando with his boxers in my laundry hamper.

"No. I feel sore in addition to being pissed off, under caffeinated and annoyed that I have to buy replacement clothes," I snapped as Carla reached the top of the staircase and looked between the two of us. "Now I can yell at both of you at the same time, though, so I do appreciate the distraction for efficiency purposes. Though I want my money back, I still feel tense."

"Just efficiency?" His smug smile did things to my lower regions that were not suitable in the presence of my sister in law. "You were not efficient, but we can try again."

"What did I miss?" She asked, giving Winnie an affectionate ear rub as she scanned the room for threats and then settled onto the armchair beside my couch. "You two do it again?"

"Aside from some jerk shooting my cell phone, threatening me and murdering Shelly? You missed the opportunity to come clean and tell me what the hell was going on before the other stuff happened! Now there's a dead sheep, I need another new phone and I have to throw away muddy, bloody and sheep urine soaked clothing!" I practically shoved the coffeemaker off the counter pressing the brew now button and she sucked her lips into her mouth to keep whatever judgment she was feeling inside. "Whether or not we 'did it' is irrelevant."

"Is she calmer now than before you screwed her or did your efforts have no effect on this?" Carla stage-whispered to Cruz and I threw a roll of paper towels at her head.

Sadly, I missed, and Winnie plucked them from the air and pranced around with her prize clutched in her teeth. I watched her leap onto my bed, drop the towels and flop onto my pillows, ears and eyes flitting around the room.

"I'm going with the latter. Maybe you should get like... a manual on the female body because she needs to relax," Carla said with a chuckle and I searched for something else to throw at her when she raised her hands in surrender. "I'm kidding! Geez, what the hell is going on?"

"I told you what the hell is going on. What did you drag me into with whatever this Conri Kade business is and how do I get out of it?" I dumped the coffee that had already brewed into my cup and chugged it without offering any to my guests. "This was a favor to search a diplomat's home for explosives. A rich man having a party that needed the reassurance of a bomb sniffing canine. Turns out he wasn't a diplomat, probably not rich and people *really* want him dead. Now it's an assignment to keep a witness from blowing the whistle on the American government and a radicalized man on a mission! Why am I involved in this? I served my country, I got the dog, and it's done."

"Technically, your discharge contract puts you in a reserve status for..." Cruz began, and I threw a balled up washcloth at him.

"Don't tell me what my contract says, Cruz. I know what it says, and if this were an official assignment requested by the government, I would do my duty. But there was no summons, no call to action..." He pulled a folded up piece of paper from his pants and I gaped at him. "Seriously? You had that in your pants the whole time and you didn't give it to me sooner?"

"I got distracted giving you other things that were in my pants," he said, walking over and handing the paper to me with an Eskimo kiss nose rub. "But... Your service is officially requested at the insistence of Conri Kade. Welcome to the Classified Information inner circle."

My eyes tracked to his lips and I felt butterflies in my stomach. Despite all the odds against it, the government wanted my help again.

Unfortunately, I didn't want to help the government.

"If you want a kiss, you can ask, Cyn," he whispered, leaning in until our mouths were nearly touching. "If you don't ask, it's now technically workplace harassment."

"Can I-" He pressed his lips to mine and I lost my anger as his tongue swirled around my mouth.

"Always," he answered, taking a step back while I tried to get the tap dancing marching band in my body to settle down.

Carla cleared her throat and I saw a folded piece of paper in her hand as well.

"Sorry to interrupt, but if these are accurate, we're in trouble. Now that I know you have one, this just got complicated."

Brows furrowed, I unfolded the paper Cruz handed me and read.

```
Attention Cynthia Sharp:

You are contractually bound to perform
the following tasks in accordance with
your military discharge contract. The
contents of this assignment and the in-
formation contained within are classified
and confidential from all parties outside
those present on the morning of August
seventeenth at the R. B. Hayes Ranch.
Should you fail to maintain the secrecy
requested, you will be brought up on
```

criminal charges with the Department of
Defense and be stripped of your military
title and privilege.

-Protect Conri Kade from explosives,
firearms and general assault. He is the
only insurance we have that American
participation in the elimination of four
experimental sites in Africa will not be
made public.

-Conduct security sweeps of all locations related to his security and
movement.

-Maintain verbal and visual contact
with all security staff members. Report
suspicious people immediately.

Below that was a seal and a bunch of names that meant
absolutely nothing to me.

"The men in the barn were right," I looked between Carla
and Cruz. "We killed those people. This whole thing is a
government CYA and they are using us to get away with it."

Carla nodded with an angry jerk of her head and Cruz
remained stoic.

"What if I refuse to help?" I asked, looking between them.
"What if I go to the press and expose the whole rotten history
that started before I was alive?"

"You'll be brought up on charges," Cruz answered, voice
flat and robotic.

"What's this loss of title and privilege business?" I asked and his eyes darted to my bed.

"They are threatening to take Winnie."

"This is crap!" I yelled, turning to the staircase when I heard the fire door at the bottom open. "Did you bug this place? Is that them?"

Cruz shook his head and produced a firearm from his waistband. We listened to the footsteps ascending the staircase and I grabbed a butcher knife from the counter while Carla pulled a weapon out of a lower back holster.

"Who's there?" I asked, my voice breaking while my eyes darted to Winnie. Her nose was working, but her body language didn't provide any clues until Stella's head popped up on the landing.

"It's me. James and I watched the films at your mom's house, and I discovered the awkward portion of watching research adult films with a man you are dating," she nodded her head once and looked at the guns held by the two other people in the room.

"Are those necessary?" Her head tilted but fear rolled off of her in waves.

Additional footsteps made their way up the stairs behind her. Carla and Cruz holstered their guns, but I kept my grip on the knife. "All of your Canadians are in there. None looked to be in distress, but I can't say for sure whether or not their participation was voluntary or coerced. I will say that if those men are indeed missing, they are certainly not missing out."

I nodded at her, but my eyes were watching the beads of sweat forming at her hairline. Winnie stood up and let out a low growl, while Stella's eyes widened.

"Who's behind you Stella?" I asked as a balding man popped up behind her with an electric cattle prod sizzling in the air. Another growl bounced around the room.

"Winnie," I warned and she laid down, but remained at the ready while the man wrapped a hand around the back of Stella's neck, pushing her forward and brandishing the prod in warning.

"Friend of yours?" I asked, eyes wide with meaning.

"No. He didn't tell me his name, but he demanded to speak with you," she swallowed around the grip on her neck and my hand clenched the knife tighter. "He kept James as insurance."

Chapter Sixteen: Reliably Unreliable

S tella's hand shook slightly, the sweat on her hairline doubling before slowly dripping down her cheek. I could see her curling her toes in and out in her shoe while her fingers stimmed on her outer thigh.

"Are you OK?" I asked her, noting that there was no blood on her clothing or noticeable signs of bruising.

"Yes. Though I admit I never anticipated I'd fall victim to the proverbial man with candy," she sighed, and I titled my head at her. "He claimed to be your friend, sent by you to collect me from your mother's house with urgent business. It was as though every stranger danger instinct I possessed was thrown out the window at the mention of your name."

"That's a first... normally people hear my name and run away," I kept my eyes on the hand wrapped on her neck. "Maybe a good strategy moving forward is to do that and call me later?"

"I tried. Your phone might be dead," her fingers picked up the tempo of their tapping without changing the pattern. Middle finger, thumb, ring, index, pinkie twice and then the order reversed.

"It's a different kind of dead than you're thinking." Her fingers paused and she was momentarily distracted. I looked between her and Cruz, trying to send a message. "Not even The Resurrection Stone can bring it back."

"Perhaps someone can make you an indestructible phone? Not adamantium because that isn't real... nor vibranium... perhaps what black boxes are made out of?"

"I'd be more inclined to switch to homing pigeons at this point," I huffed, watching her body calm. As long as Stella didn't panic, we'd figure something out. "Cleaning up after them would be a dick, but at least if one gets shot there would be back-ups and bird food is probably cheap."

"This isn't social hour, losers," Baldy spat and my eyes went to his face, hand tightening on the blade in my hand. The movement traveled through my whole arm and pulled his attention. "Drop the knife, Cynthia."

"Or what?" I challenged, looking for a crack in his mask. I needed a weakness to exploit, then presumably Cruz and Carla would jump into action. Nothing says poorly constructed plan like hoping people will read your mind and take action without discussing it previously.

"Or we find out why cattle prods are illegal substitutes to tasers." His sneer was accompanied by another electrical demonstration before he shoved the prod into her ribs. The move elicited a whimper and I almost ran to her.

So much for calming stories of distraction.

"OK, fine," I said, releasing the knife and walking to the cabinet.

"What the hell are you doing?" He shouted and I blinked at him before pulling out a coffee mug.

"Drinking coffee. You want some?" I asked, glancing back into the cabinet to confirm the prong taser I kept on the shelf was charged and ready. The trick was going to be getting him far enough away from Stella to keep her body from becoming part of the circuit.

"Are you not listening? I told you not to move!" He was getting agitated, but his grip on her remained steady. Whatever his objective, he had the skills to follow through on it.

Unfortunate, since most of my experience was un-skilled muscle with limited intelligence.

It had been a long time since I stood against someone who knew what they were doing.

"You told me to put down the knife. You didn't say I needed to stay still, a virtual impossibility for me. You also did not say I couldn't have coffee, a reasonable decision if you or anyone you work with has met me. Everyone knows that if I don't have coffee, I become unpleasant," I pulled out cups for Carla and Cruz to clear the path to the taser behind it. With the cup I'd already drunk from, there were four cups on the counter, and I had to hope he didn't notice or think I would ever share my coffee with him.

"You definitely should allow her to drink the coffee," Stella confirmed at the same time Cruz and Carla both responded.

"You're less dangerous than her without coffee."

"Please, are you trying to get us all killed?"

It was both mortifying and amusing with a touch of insanity. My face broke into a deranged smile, eyes going wide to emphasize the underlying madness before collapsing back into blank indifference.

I should have skipped the Army and been an actor.

"What the hell is wrong with you all?" He snapped, looking between all the captives in the room and moving Stella more squarely in front of him. It wasn't much of a crack, but it was something. He couldn't handle crazy people.

I pulled the coffee pot out of the maker and poured it into three of the four cups in front of me including the one I'd finished just after Carla had arrived. Then I turned to the fridge for a splash of milk and peppermint syrup.

"There are conflicting hypotheses on that, but the most consensus-y answer I have is 'a lot' and it's best to roll with it." I shrugged and raised my mug to him. "Suffice to say, without this I will jeopardize everyone and everything to destroy what stands in my way of consuming it."

My eyes didn't break contact with him while I drank and I watched Cruz retrieve his gun and slide it under his thigh on the couch. Carla was dead center in the room, shifting to draw attention away from Cruz.

"Well you have your coffee, come out of the kitchen and sit on the floor," he jabbed Stella harder with the prod and I raised my empty hand in surrender.

So much for the taser.

"Geez, chill," I grabbed one of the other two cups I poured and offered it to Carla. "Why don't you start with your name and ease into your super villain rant? You can't expect us to display the appropriate level of fear if we don't know what we're supposed to be afraid of."

I sat cross-legged on the floor beside the chair and placed Carla's mug in front of her, trying to discreetly check the underside of my coffee table for my stun gun. It was taped closer to Cruz and I wasn't going to be able to reach it.

Damn-it, I need more weapons, I scowled into my cup of coffee before drinking it in six gulps while he continued.

If I were willing to waste coffee, it would be an excellent weapon but I was hoping it wouldn't come to that. Throwing hot coffee and breaking mugs was not a habit I wanted to get into.

"This isn't a rant, it's a warning. You're messing with things you have no business meddling in. Protect yourself and your loved ones and walk away!" He gestured the cattle prod at me on the floor. Instinct and annoyance kicked in, sending my arm out and ripping it from his hand.

I felt Carla shift uncomfortably beside me.

"Great. What business am I walking away from?" I asked, tossing the cattle prod on the bed and then wishing I hadn't when he produced a knife. It happened in a blink, his arm retracted, and it was suddenly holding a knife against Stella's collarbone.

She was probably in less danger from the cattle prod and I screwed up.

"Are you done playing the hero or do you need another warning?" He pressed the sharp edge of the blade into her skin until a droplet of blood pooled and dripped onto the knife.

"I get it," I held my hands in surrender. Her pupils were fully dilated and everything about her breathing and posture said in another minute she would pass out. The young woman was not equipped to be a hostage. She was barely equipped to walk into a shopping mall during the holidays. "Continue with your warning."

I set my empty cup down and switched it for Carla's untouched one. I took a long drink and circled my finger on the rim, trying to get Stella to follow my finger and calm down. I watched her breathe, her eyes following my finger turned into her index tracing a circle of its own on her thigh.

"Look, whatever you're doing, just stop it. Stop looking, stop running around, just sit and stay here. Leave it all alone! There are secrets that need to be told and this is how it's funded! We can't let this stand, not anymore!"

I choked on the gulp of coffee in my throat. Was he here about Conri or the missing Canadians?

His grip relaxed on the knife and Cruz surged to his feet. Stella was thrown at me, the knife slicing toward Cruz's arm and leaving red trails along his arm. The man had rotated toward the stairs and started running down them.

"Shoot him!" I yelled at Cruz, but his eyes betrayed his intention. Though he'd pulled the gun out, he was not planning on using it unless our lives were threatened. Perhaps not even then if the injury wouldn't be fatal.

He wanted the man for reasons his blank expression wouldn't betray and I felt once again he had an objective he hadn't shared with the rest of us.

"Damn-it," I shoved to my feet, verifying Carla had Stella and ran after both men as Cruz started down the stairs. Our pounding footsteps echoed off the concrete walls and the adrenaline let down of the past twenty minutes caught up with me. We burst through the bottom fire door only seconds after the man to find a green pick-up truck with country music blasting from the window. A back door opened, James was shoved out onto the ground and it roared down the alley while Cruz memorized the plate and started after it.

"Where's your Jeep?" He asked and I pointed the opposite direction of the truck. "Crap."

He jogged faster after the truck, reaching the end of the alley long after they turned and pulling his phone out to make a call. I wasn't certain where he had parked but I had a feeling it was just as far away as my vehicle and he didn't think he could make it to either in time to catch the men in the green truck, but I had an idea where to find them.

"You OK?" I asked James, removing the flexi cuffs from his wrists and checking the scrapes on his arms and cheek.

"Yeah..." He groaned as he tried to sit up and cut the flex cuffs off his ankle with a knife he had in his back pocket. "Stella?"

"I'm fine. Though I may have a meltdown later and I'm going to request you try to understand that whatever I say it is about, it's probably really about this. Why are you on the ground?" Their eyes met and I saw affection flowing both ways before his eyes caught on her neck.

"I got thrown out of a car. What the hell happened?" She blinked at his question and swiped at the dried blood on her neck. "I'm going to kill him. Do you need stitches? Should we go to the clinic?"

"I believe it has healed. The man threatened me with a knife, but it doesn't hurt, now or when he did it. Should we re-watch the films?" Stella asked me and I felt James stiffen beside me. "I don't know how else to help and I'm not quite ready to process this yet. We could perhaps experiment some? I'm not certain I'm fully ready to..."

"Shhh... Stella, after today, I'm really only down for cuddling and pizza. Besides, I don't think we have access to the films anymore and they were disturbing enough the first time."

We looked at him as Cruz made his way closer. I watched James shift, eyes darting toward the man as he walked. If body language was accurate, he was hoping to prevent Cruz from hearing anything he shared.

"Jake, the guy in the car, called someone and ordered them to get the discs back. Said they royally screwed up and no one was supposed to see the films. Called them a bunch of horny old bitches," he got quieter the closer Cruz got. "They said their inside man couldn't keep 'her' distracted forever but the only 'hers' mentioned were you and Carla. Do you trust that guy? Is he... I mean... do you find him... distracting?"

Studying his face, I pressed my lips together before looking intently at Cruz as he arrived beside me, sliding an arm around my waist. The instant shot of heat that went through my body said I was definitely distracted. Even traumatic hostage situations couldn't keep me from wanting to lick his neck.

Not that I did, but the impulse was strong.

Did I trust him?

It was a question that haunted me since we drove through a wall in Afghanistan.

Could I trust him?

I looked at his face, and back between the two twenty-year-olds in front of me.

No, the answer was simple. He had his own agenda every time I worked with him. Every time, he would put everyone else in danger to meet his goals. A better question was, whose side was he on this time?

Chapter
Seventeen: Chilly

"**D**o you want me to leave?" Cruz asked, his hand running up and down my arm, but I couldn't relax. We were sitting at my mother's house for Sunday dinner, an event I only recently received an invitation to. Though the couch was newer than some of the other furniture, it still felt foreign to sit on it beside Cruz.

He really didn't belong here, but he was sitting beside me as though we normally had family dinner with my parents, my brother and his demonic children. Cruz was a chameleon who fit in everywhere, but even in places I belonged I still managed to feel like an outcast.

I was starting to question if I was switched at adolescence and he was the one who grew up in this house.

"It's up to you," I answered, staring straight ahead at the TV. It was a commercial for erectile dysfunction and I had no good excuse at the ready for why I was staring at it. My mind had been racing since James had told me what he overheard in the alley. "Everyone knows you do whatever you want to do anyway."

"Are you going to tell me what's wrong?" He asked and I shrugged his arm off, moving away to look directly at him. Ian's brown eyes were mesmerizing, but I couldn't see anything in them. While I hadn't expected him to become easier to read over time, I'd thought after our time together I would see something, feel something, besides lust and confusion. Instead, I just saw a man sitting comfortably in a place he had never been before like he'd done this every day. Every look lacked the affection exchanged between Stella and James, was void of concern over what we'd survived today, and could shine with lust as easily as they could disguise everything beneath the surface of his mind.

Nothing about being with him was easy, but it felt *good*.

When my mom had heard Stella and James had been taken after watching porn in her basement, she'd thought it was code for sneaking off to hook up. Presented with the information that they were two grown adults who did not need to sneak, she said it was a matter of personal discretion. The neighbors swore a green truck had forced them into it, but there wasn't any screaming.

My mom insisted no one was kidnapped if there wasn't any screaming.

Her same reasoning applied to orgasms, murder, and BDSM. Though she was aware Stella had concerns regarding the cleanliness and forced proximity of the act in question, she thought perhaps she was ready to go all the way. A belief that was shattered when she called me and saw blood on Stella's neck and ordered all of us to her house for dinner.

"If that man had pressed the knife harder, would you have killed him to save Stella?" I asked, studying his face. "Or would you have stood by and watched while he slit her throat?"

"Cyn, do you think I would let something bad happen to you or your friends?"

"You didn't answer my question, Ian. Answer the question I asked!" His face scrunched in pain and confirmed my fear. "You knew they were looking for me. You knew they were trying to find me or get to me, and you chose to prioritize your job of following them to their end game rather than save my life or the lives of the people I love."

"No, I would never let anything bad happen to you." His voice had grown quieter and he wasn't making eye contact. "I would have stopped him from hurting any of you."

"Except he did hurt Stella! He hurt Stella and James, and now she's about to have a breakdown and he has bruises on his wrists and ankles," I hissed the second part when my mom popped out to look at us. When we remained silent, she gave me a quick nod and slipped back into the kitchen.

My brother had Carla and his kids in the backyard, letting them scare off pigeons, solicitors and serial killers. James and Stella were helping my mom in the kitchen, which was code for she spiked their tea with rum to help them relax. I'd heard loud giggling coming from the kitchen and knew that though they were both too young to drink by a few months, they were well and truly sauced. Somewhere upstairs, my dad was trying to unearth an artifact that would amuse and delight us all through what was bound to be an intense dinner.

"It's my job, Cyn. I can't just change the rules when I don't like them." It was his turn to stare intently at the TV while he spoke. The universe must have a twisted sense of humor because now it was a tampon commercial.

"Why don't you shove a tampon up your butt to stop all the crap leaking out of it and get out my parents house," I shoved his arm, but he didn't move. "Being here, fraternizing with civilians, isn't part of your job. If what we did in the shower was part of your job, thanks for your service. You can expect your payment in six to eight weeks."

"Can't we talk about this? You have survived more life-threatening situations than any normal person. I know you can handle yourself, there's nothing to worry about when it comes to you, you can survive anything." He didn't look away and pulled me against him. "I learned not to freak out when you're in danger because you're always in danger."

"So, it's OK to put the people I love in danger because I'm always in danger? That's great, Cruz. Next you're going to tell me that women deserve to get eaten by vampires because they're always bleeding and anyone nearby is just collateral damage. That no one should help them because it's just what they deserve in the name of your job?" I punctuated every question by hitting Cruz in the arm, spitting the word *job* like it was the dirtiest word in the English language. "If the government tells you to murder me, are you going to do it? Are you going to start killing people just because they tell you? I realize that's how war works, that they tell you who the bad guy is and you point and shoot, but even a grunt knows when to cease fire. Do you exercise any independent judgment, or are you the perfect Stepford soldier?"

"It's my job, it's what I signed up for and I'm good at it," Cruz dropped his gaze to his hands, not bothering to stop me from hitting him. "This is the only thing I know how to do."

"Well, then go have dinner with your job, Ian," I shoved him harder, but he still didn't move. "If that's all you care about then you don't belong here. If that's all you know how to do, then go do it. I don't need your pity sex or your fake friendship."

Something wet and warm trickled down my face and I swiped it with the back of my hand.

Crying. I was freaking crying over *another* man.

It was like *Groundhog Day*, no matter how many times I lived through the day, the cycle just kept going. I'd never be enough, never be wanted or accepted without something else coming first.

It was time for me to let go.

"Cyn..." He reached for my jaw and I shoved his hand away. When he tried again, I slapped him across the face before standing up. "Can't you just..."

"No. I can't," I told him, walking away. "Thank you for partnering me with my best friend, Sgt. Cruz. I'll always appreciate that you brought us together, but I think it's time to go our separate ways."

It was the second time I looped my block, and the light in my apartment was still on when I knew I had turned it off.

"What do you think, girl? Friend or foe?" I asked Winnie, though her response was a wide yawn that ended in a high-pitched squeak. A shadow moved across the window and I watched the curtains creep to the side, revealing a tall figure standing at my window.

"Nope, not today," I muttered, pulling from the curb and pointing my car to the outskirts of town. "Mo has a couch. We will sleep at Mo's and in the morning..."

I pulled the Jeep back to the curb.

"In the morning someone else could have gone in and gotten hurt because I didn't go inside," I smacked my forehead on the steering wheel, willing it to have a different answer. Willing my brain to just this once say *nah, I'm good.*

Just this once, prioritize my own health and safety over hypothetical others.

"How am I not dead yet?" I muttered, circling the block and parking on a side street. My mom had sent me home with three pounds of left overs that she swore was not because I looked sad after Larry and then Cruz.

If it hadn't been smothered in melted cheese, I might have refused her. As it was, I never turned down melted cheese, cheese powder coated snacks, sandwich cookies of all flavors and gummy bears that don't cause diarrhea. None of these negated the truth.

I was, in fact, sad.

Winnie and I walked through the alley, my eyes on the lookout for green pick-ups or ski masks, but the night was quiet. The gentle hum of crickets under the light of a waning moon was peaceful. If not for the man in my window, I may have sat outside and let the evening calm my nerves.

Instead, I unlocked the back door and shared a look with my best friend. Her satellite ears were pointed straight ahead in full alert activation.

"Who's going in first?" I asked her and she scented the air. Once, twice, her head tilted before she let out a soft bark and scrambled up the stairs. Her claws clattered on the threadbare carpet, the sound bouncing off the concrete walls before the transition to drywall halfway up.

She barked twice, something heavy crashed to the floor and she barked again.

"Winnie?" I called, waiting for her head to pop out over the top of the stairs. She appeared with a nightstick in her mouth, tail wagging.

"What the hell?" I climbed up the stairs and flipped on the light. Laying half under my coffee table was Daniel Kirby. His shirt was disheveled, gun belt missing a night stick, and if I didn't know what his face looked like, I'd have thought he was laughing.

"Hey," he said from the floor, Winnie dumping his nightstick on his crotch and using his wince to go for the neck. Her teeth gently nipped at him, tail and butt in the air as she pounced in a half circle going for his neck. "Can you help me with her?"

Officer Daniel Kirby was laughing and playing with my dog.

"Winnie, place." She obeyed the command, grabbing the nightstick and trotting back toward me to sit. "What are you doing here?"

Daniel hauled himself off the floor and straightened out his shirt.

"Carla told me about earlier..." he looked around nervously and I arched my brow in his direction. "She asked me to check out your house and keep it safe until you got home from dinner. She also might have ordered me to stock your fridge with ice cream and cans of frosting though I admittedly didn't do that because I didn't want you to vomit on my boots. I did bring you something I thought you needed"

I nodded and looked down at Winnie. Gripping the end closest to me, I took hold of his nightstick and waited for her to look at me.

"Out," I ordered, and she released the stick so I could hand it back to Daniel.

"Thanks. This is for you," he handed me a cellphone that looked a couple of years old. It still has a finger ID button at the bottom and I was grateful not to have anything new to destroy. "I had it activated with your number, but you'll have to load your contacts into it. Been going off since they turned it on, though half of the messages are my brother."

"Thanks," I said, flipping the computer around in my hand and smiling at the pink color. "Carla?"

"No, it's an old phone I had lying around. Well, it belonged to my wife, and when Larry said he tried calling you, Carla told me what happened to your last phone. Thought maybe I could help." His words turned his ears a pinkish color and his eyes remained firmly locked over my left ear while his feet shuffled nervously. "I need to tell you something, though."

"OK," I answered, looking at the six voicemails and dozens of text notifications sitting on the device. None of the contacts were labeled, so I quickly scanned the summary of the voice messages and the text previews. "You weren't joking about Larry. Where did you get the picture?"

His number was the only one with a contact name and a picture of us as kids assigned to it.

"It's on the wall in my mom's house, thought you might as well have something in there before you filled it up with pictures of your dog."

"Thanks. Surprised she put it up. What did you want to tell me?" I asked before we could get lost wandering down memory lane.

"Right. I read what one of the voicemails said. Robin? She's having a baby, or at least that's what the message said when she started shouting at a man about pickle butter cookie dough. I know her, or knew her, it's been awhile since she's gone to the bar we hang at. We would talk about friends and family in Canada while sharing beers and catching up on the CHL and NHL. Her brother, Noah... She spent months going on about how she was trying to get him in the country where she could keep an eye on him after he got flogged in public for shagging a woman's husband, her words though I have no idea where the London slang came from, she'd never been as far as I know. We were both regulars at a hockey bar way out in the middle of nowhere. When she figured out how to get her brother in, she passed the info to me and I gave it to my cousin. When Robin told me she'd finally found someone who could help, I'd immediately thought it would ease the burden on my cousin's family. I gave my cousin all of the information and she said everything was set up," he swallowed and met my eyes. "I know you already know that both Noah and my cousin are gone, but there was another man. Richard Johnson, this bigger guy with a beer belly and an obsession with flannel, he heard us one night and we gave him the info too. I'm worried his brother might be the next one to go missing."

"John Jack Johnson?" I asked, pressing my fingers into my temple. "John Johnson has a brother named Dick Johnson? What a cruel family..."

Daniel laughed for a second before scratching his neck.

"Yeah, how did you know?" He asked, studying my face. "Did you meet him? Is he safe?"

"He's already gone, but I think I know where all of them ended up. They're safe... for the most part... Though I'm not sure how they'll feel when we find them. This bar called The Ice Box? Had a minor explosion and car fire there the other day?"

"Damn! That was you?" Daniel looked mildly impressed but I shook my head.

"Nope. Just a bystander, but I got to the bar on the back of that van. Any of the times you were there, did you see a green pick-up or anyone who looked a little too interested in your conversations? Before or after you got the information about the immigration service?" I asked, watching his mind parse through the question and pair it with what I assumed were drunken memories.

"There was this one guy, he worked there. Looked like a barback? Maybe a short order cook? Nasty little dude who looks like he bathes once a year and it's in bacon grease. Caught him peeing in the alley more than once and itching his junk in the middle of the room," he rubbed his chin and thought for a long moment. "There might have been a green truck... but I can't say for sure. Wait, did you just say you know where they are?"

I nodded and checked the clock on my microwave. It would be nearly ten when I got there, but it was worth a look around. Sleep was unlikely and a busy mind is my personal favorite cure to a broken heart.

"They are being forced to act in porn with old ladies. Stella confirmed the faces matched and the known tattoos, I just don't know where they operate other than 'locally' according to my mom," I shrugged off my hoodie and walked to the metal rod that served as a makeshift closet. Grabbing a long sleeve shirt and a clean pair of cargos, I went into the bathroom and changed out of my sweats.

"Where are you going?" He asked, watching me pull on socks. Winne was curled up with her head on my pillow and looked unwilling to go back out tonight. Apparently taking the nightstick toy was the last straw and she was going night night.

"To give an unsanitary man a yellow card with a ten-yard penalty. If the bar is the only place all of you intersect, it's worth taking a look and asking questions. Do you want to come with me?"

"You... that's... those aren't even the same sport!" He choked on a laugh and I shrugged. "Seriously, have you ever watched a game of anything?"

"I watched *Remember the Titans* and *A League of Their Own*, does that count?"

"No, geez." He laughed and put his arm on my shoulder. "Do you know the difference between football, baseball, soccer and hockey?"

"One of them only exists in America and the rest use sticks?" I grabbed my keys and he shook his head. "Except the panda ball which has the pokey shoes and you can't use your hands unless you get stuck in the net?"

Daniel plucked the keys from my hand and led me down the stairs.

"I'll drive, you need to Google sports before you get your ass kicked."

Chapter Eighteen: Into the Woods

I t was almost two hours later when we arrived at the bar.

Daniel had needed to go back to the station to change out of his uniform. On the way there, he was flagged down by a citizen who swore there was an intruder in her backyard and ran out the front door to escape before being raped and or murdered, her words. The rapist/murderer had crawled in low to the ground and was discovered when he knocked over every alloy trashcan in her backyard.

The deputy took her seriously and investigated the situation.

Personally, I had felt it more likely Ms. Katz took a few too many sleeping pills and wouldn't remember this in the morning. It wasn't a baseless assumption since two months ago she swore an alligator was swimming up her drain pipe and tried to go swimming in her neighbor's bird bath to get the "feeling of scales" off.

Gun drawn and flashlight out, Daniel approached her house in full on Dudley Do-Right mode. After he had me wait with the woman at the end of the street, he crept tactically toward her house, pausing to listen every few feet. It would have been comical how hard he was trying when he searched the area, but I was trying to cut back on my mockery of the man. It was one thing to mock him while dating his brother, since that made him practically family, but now that we were broken up...

I was saved from my train of thought when Daniel burst through the wooden gate at full speed. Arms flailing, feet moving quickly and he couldn't stop screaming.

"Raccoons!" His shouting could be heard over half the town over. "There are so many raccoons!"

He and the sleeping pill addicted resident had run off together and it took fifteen minutes to calm them both down enough to move on. Ms. Katz was coaxed back to bed with a promise that raccoons couldn't unlock her back door with a bobby pin. Daniel got back in his patrol car and headed to the station to change and write a report that would conveniently leave out the running and screaming.

Not that it mattered, I'd already posted the video on YouTube.

But all of that had cost us an hour and I was already regretting my decision to take off my sweats and leave the house. I was far too old to be this far away from my bed late at night.

"So, what's the plan?" He asked, leaning against the steering wheel and eyeing the front of the bar. "Are we trying to blend or demanding answers?"

"Do whatever you want. After the raccoon incident I'm not going to be seen with you in public," I answered, climbing out of the passenger side of my Jeep. He passed me my keys as we rounded our separate sides and met at the front of the vehicle.

"Come on! Those things look like burglars and old west bandits! You'd have run screaming too!" He insisted, stomping his feet to the front of the bar while I loitered casually a few feet away.

"Be that as it may, I'm waiting at least sixty seconds to go in after you and if there's another option, I'm not sitting next to you," I insisted, leaning casually against the front grill of my car. Daniel smirked, hopped the railing in front of the bar and landed in front of me. "Impressive. Still not going in there *with* you, Tigger."

"Don't be so sure," he mocked, gripping my bicep, pulling me against him before squatting down and forcing my body to fold at the waist around his shoulder.

A very undignified scream passed through my lips and he pushed up with his legs.

Something popped in his back. Then it was his turn to scream and I landed on top of him on the filthy asphalt. Tears pooled at the corners of his eyes and he had gone red in the face grimacing against the pain.

"I've seen Larry and Cruz pick you up," he whined, and I laughed. "You don't look that fat!"

"They work out... kind of. You've gone soft Deputy Daniel," I climbed off of him and offered him a hand. "Also, I am that fat and you just proved why it's a good thing! I'm hard to kidnap and if you were a real bad guy, you'd be incapacitated until help arrived."

"I work out," he sulked, ignoring my hand.

"Baby making cardio isn't a real fitness activity," I countered and he flinched when I gripped his bicep.

"I think I just need to lay here for a minute," his voice cracked and I shook my head, grabbing his other arm and hauling him to his feet before wrapping an arm around his torso to support his weight.

"Much as it would amuse me to watch you lay in a parking lot and take bets on which car will run over your head and scatter the contents of your skull like a smashed watermelon..." He gaped at me with a strangled gurgle and I smiled brightly. "Come on, you know you'd do the same."

"I would not! I would help you after you *almost* got run over!" His childish tone forced a laugh out of me as I got us to the door of the bar.

"I didn't say I'd let them smash your watermelon head, only that I'd take bets on who'd manage it first," I responded and pushed the door open expecting another record scratching moment of silence.

Instead, it was a relatively calm scene of men lined up on barstools watching sports. All eyes were glued to the screens lining the rear of the bar, and the men who were seated at tables had their eyes trained to more TVs that faced different parts of the room. On Friday night, I hadn't really taken the time to look around. Now that I did, I wished I hadn't.

Ripped green pleather booths rimmed three fourths of the room. In the center were about four tables with chairs and the barstools I'd sat on the other night looked sticky and oddly shiny for something that wasn't made of metal.

"Catastrophe Chick!" A man yelled out and I checked out the bar.

Beardy was working again and he looked a little too happy to see me. While my pain free body noticed his tattoos and lip piercings under a tight black tee, I still wasn't a huge fan of being Catastrophe Chick.

Accuracy aside, my name was alliterative enough without the nickname.

"What happened to him? Did you kick his ass?" His wide smile was contagious and a few of the men at the bar turned around to look at Daniel. The deputy smiled weakly and offered a half wave before I deposited him into a booth in the back corner.

"Nah. Old man tried to do fitness and threw out his back. Got any anti-inflammatories?" I asked, walking up to the bar and glancing through the pass-through window at the open kitchen door.

"Only medicines I've got are Jim, Jack, Tito and Jose," he smirked to Daniel who had laid out across the bench. "That man only drinks beer though and I'm pretty sure that makes you retain water."

"Great, give him an Irish Car Bomb. Best of both worlds," I was proud of my drop-shot booze compromise. There weren't any sounds coming from the kitchen area and I leaned back to look down the hallway with the phone and the bathroom. All eyes were glued to the screens and tense muscles said no one was moving until this pivotal moment of sports had passed.

I wondered if they'd look at me if I walked around topless.

"What are you looking for?" He asked, pulling a pint of Guinness and setting it on the wooden countertop.

"Shorty. I think his unsanitary behavior gave me Giardia and I want to kick his ass before swabbing him to grow a culture and identify his exact strain of filth."

It was a lie, but I saw Dick Johnson sitting at the bar and he was watching me closely. I wasn't ready to tell him his brother was an adult film actor yet... or that I thought Shorty had arranged to profit off of it. Beardy poured the shot of Jameson and Baileys, and I looked directly at Dick who turned bright red and turned away. My eyes went back to Beardy who had a shit-eating grin on his face.

"Shorty? You mean the alley pisser? His name is Greg and he's on a break. But if you need a friend, Johnson over there has had a bit of a crush on you since you stuck your face in his lap," Beardy whispered, passing me the two glasses and I put a twenty on the bar. "Pretty sure if you touched him, he'd get off in his jeans."

Beardy got my disgusted face and I considered scolding him.

"Dude, even if that's true, don't tell people that. Makes you look like a perv. When is the pisser back from his break?"

He checked the clock on the wall and then the score on the TV.

"Probably another twenty minutes." He snickered and I carried the glasses over to Daniel who hadn't moved.

"Sit up, old man, and drink this," I set the cups in front of him and he groaned.

"I'm not old!" His pouting lips made me want to offer him a clean diaper, but I refrained. "What is this?"

"Irish Car Bomb. Drop the shot in the beer and chug," I explained, eyes still scanning the room. Sliding into the booth opposite the prostrate man, I counted five men at the bar and three tables with at least two men. Despite not being a large bar, it was decently busy for a Sunday night. The air smelled like sweat and stale beer, but there was no fried food or burnt meat. "Why did you order me this?"

The old man had managed a seated position and was eyeing the cups like they contained poison.

"Because you're in pain. This will knock you on your ass, but since you're already there, you might as well be there in slightly less pain. Now drop and chug, man. I know you're old and probably have acid reflux and an occasional touch of the vapors..."

He kicked me under the table to stop and took the drink with a grimace on his face. Halfway through the pint he choked and swallowed hard before coughing loudly for at least a minute. All eyes in the bar turned to us and I shook my head at him.

"Real smooth, Kirby," I muttered, watching the shadows behind the bar. We still had half the patron's attention, but I wasn't looking for a date. "Finish your drink and try to look like a tough guy before I have to punch someone to protect your virtue."

"You poisoned me!" He hissed and I saw Beardy smirk at his red face and watering eyes.

"Geez, how did I ever think you were hot," I muttered, grabbing the rest of his drink and finishing it in two swallows. "Now put your reading glasses on and help me look for the dirty little man."

"I don't wear reading glasses!" He huffed, but carefully got to his feet and approached the bar. Despite not finishing his medicine, he was moving a little better. All of the muscles above his lower back were moving stiffly, but he was moving on his own and that was progress.

On the screens above us, the little black dot bounced back and forth across the ice. The movement was soothing and mesmerizing, everyone in the bar tense as they waited for it to glide into the butterfly net trap.

"Drink this," he said, setting a glass in front of me. I eyed the cup and gave it a cursory sniff.

"Is this just a beer?" I asked, taking a cautious sip and shrugging before drinking half of it. It had a cinnamon-y apple taste that made me think it was sparkling cider. "It's good."

"It's hard cider," he took a long drink of his own.

Movement in the corner of the room caught my attention and I tuned out Daniel's response. Amid the chaos of cheering and boos as a team scored, there was another sound. A waterfall, maybe, or a running tap that leaked onto the floor. Curiosity pulled me out of my seat and I moved along the wall toward where I'd seen the shadow of a man.

"Where are you going?" Daniel whispered in my ear and I shuddered at his proximity.

"Dude, back up," I grumbled quietly and saw the shadow sat just beyond the slightly propped back door. We walked toward it cautiously, the waterfall sound getting louder and reaching a climax as I pushed on the door and stepped out into the night.

And straight into a puddle of piss.

"Again? Are you kidding me?" I whipped my head around and glared at the short man in the apron. "There's a bathroom in there! I realize the employee bathroom is less than ideal, but there is a real one, for customers! This is the second time I've had your urine on my shoes and I'm considering kicking it back at you."

"W-what are you doing here?" Real fear shone in Greg's eyes and I cocked my head to the side in confusion.

"I was looking for you," I started before his eyes went wide and he turned around to sprint away with his pants undone. "Don't run!"

My shout was lost in the night as my feet thundered after him. We passed the hollowed out carcass of the blue van and cut down a dirt shoulder between the road and a chain link fence. Despite being short, pudgy and confident urinating in public, the man was fast and I pushed myself to run faster.

I nearly lost him when he reached a tree line of conifers and picked his way carefully between the exposed roots. My height was a disadvantage, eyes struggling to tell my feet where to go when my face kept getting smacked with branches. Nearly ready to give up, I stumbled out onto a hard-packed trail and Shorty Greg was bent over huffing and puffing for air.

"Can you stop now?" I shouted, and his wide eyes showed me he planned to run. "Come on! Please?"

He bolted and I let out a labored sigh.

"This is getting old!" I shouted after him, picking up speed and rounding the bend shortly after he did only to be blinded by an LED light flooding the area. "What the..."

A howling moan cut through the night, then the lights flashed and the light blinked lime green. When I tried to move closer, small pinpricks of resistance pushed back against me as I tried to fight my way forward through what felt like a sea of military grade spider webs.

"Cyn!" Daniel was panting behind me. I turned for a second and a freezing liquid poured down my back as another howling screech of pleasure reverberated through the woods. Daniel grabbed the back of my shirt and pulled me out of the way of a falling tree branch. "We'll come back in the morning!"

Fighting free of his hand, I tried to go forward when my foot caught something on the ground and it coiled around my ankle with barbed spikes that bit into my flesh.

"Damn it!" I howled as another beastly cry came from the illuminated clearing and a thundering herd of footsteps charged toward us. "Shit, run!"

I pulled my foot hard and felt my skin rip under my pants leg, but I was free. Stumbling in pain like a drunken peg-leg pirate, Daniel and I fought our way through the brush and tree roots to fall out of the woods into the parking lot of the bar.

"What the hell was that?" Daniel shouted but I could only shrug, marveling at how the lights had disappeared as easily as we'd stumbled on them.

"No idea. But I'll have to find out tomorrow in the light of day," I muttered, staggering to my feet and looking down at my blood-soaked ankle. "Could you take me somewhere that gives stitches and tetanus shots?"

Chapter Nineteen: Invasion of the Suits

There was no good time to get up after a night in the emergency room. If there were a good time, it would certainly not be six in the morning. Though I'd wanted to go back out to the bar and see the booby-trapped woods in the light of the day, a voicemail from Joseph thwarted my plans. The message insisted I needed to handle the morning shift at the dairy for a while if I wanted to keep my job.

The manager's promise that Larry wouldn't be there was just an added bonus to regular income.

"Quad shot," I croaked to Mo who was diligently preparing pastries for her opening in twenty minutes. Though I'd managed to stagger to my Jeep and drive it to her shop a quarter mile away without further injury, it took all my energy and I collapsed onto a stool she kept in the corner. "With extra caffeine and six times the recommended amount of sugar."

Though I had made and consumed an entire pot of coffee before leaving my apartment, it had been defective. The toasty bean water had barely made a dent in the resistance my eyelids had to opening. It was time to bring in the hard stuff... Italian crack water.

"Why are you limping?" Mo asked, taking in my disheveled appearance.

"Barbed wire booby trap," I said, lifting my pant leg to show the bandage on my ankle. It didn't need stitches, but the amount of grime they cleaned out meant that I had to get a hepatitis shot in addition to tetanus and one that was either for Bubonic Plague, mad cow disease or rabies. Either way, the bandage was waterproof and I'd taken an hour-long shower when Daniel dropped me off with my Jeep. He then staggered to Larry's house to crash on the couch to avoid "his wife's bellyaching".

"Espresso?"

She inclined her head to a machine that belonged on the Starship Enterprise.

"That carafe next to it is Americano. I ran out of dark roast and my supplier has it on backorder. So I've just been serving watered down espresso in its place," she talked without looking up from the bread she was braiding and coating in butter and herbs.

"Thank you," I hissed, getting to my feet and hobbling across the room to a stainless steel counter. On the way, I passed a tray of cooling muffins and stuffed one in my mouth. "Hot!"

Mo cackled and offered me a spoonful of cool frosting.

"That's what you get for trying to steal food. You know I'll always feed you," she set my muffin aside and handed me something with jelly and custard in a flaky crust. "Eat this while that cools and get your coffee."

I took a huge bite and let out a soft moan.

"Thanks," I grumbled, carrying it to the machine. I poured an unreasonable amount of liquid into an oversized glass measuring cup I declared suitable for my caffeination needs. Beside the dispenser was a fridge and I pulled out something that looked dairy adjacent and dumped it into the two quart dish with white powder from the counter.

Unfortunately, it had been buttermilk and baking soda.

"Eck!" I spat, but didn't stop drinking even as I fought back a gag. Mo took my measuring cup pitcher to sniff it and made a face that rivaled mine when cleaning up Winnie poop.

"What did you do?" She asked, trying to carry my beverage to the sink and dump it out.

"No! I need it!" I cried, taking it back from her and choking it down in a few gulps. Once I forced back the first gag reflex, my throat just accepted its punishment and kept swallowing.

The occupational possibilities with such a skill were not lost on me, but I wasn't so inclined.

"Oh my god, Cyn, there's more coffee! You don't need to..." but she let out a sigh and rinsed my measuring pitcher. She refilled it with more coffee and correctly put sweetened condensed milk, honey crystals, and raw sugar into it. I took two sips and moaned in pleasure.

"I love you, will you ditch Chris and be mine?" I asked her and she offered me a half-smile.

"I love you too, but no," she pointed a spatula toward the back door and I turned to see Ian Cruz standing in her doorway with dark circles under his eyes and wrinkled clothing that might be the same as what he had on yesterday. "You want me to bake him into something for you?"

Tilting my head in consideration, I wondered what he'd taste like as a muffin.

Or maybe one of those pink breads they sold at Vallarta.

"Chica, can we talk?" He asked and I shook my head.

"Gotta go to work," I said around my last gulp of coffee before putting the measuring cup in the sink and grabbing my now cool muffin. Now that it wasn't scalding my tongue, I was fairly certain it was some sort of apple oatmeal deal. "Thanks my love, even if you won't dump Chris for me, you're the best."

Mo gave me a hug and another spoonful of frosting.

"There's cheese bagels by the door," she offered, and I grabbed one. "Text me later."

"You got it," I walked out the back door and Cruz followed, watching me walk with an angry glint in his eyes. "Do you have a problem, Sgt.? Do you really think she'd offer you a cheese bagel after yesterday?"

"What happened to your ankle?" His hand snatched my pant leg and pulled it up to reveal the bandage. "What did you do last night?"

"You are oddly forceful for someone who acknowledges I'm 'always in danger'. Last night I tried to find some missing Canadians," I snapped at him, pulling my pants out of his hand and stomping to my Jeep where Winnie poked her head out and gave me a kiss that reminded me, I was wearing crumbs.

"By yourself?" His hand held my door closed and I resisted the urge to punch him.

"Not that it's any of your business, but I took Daniel."

Stomping on his foot, he was just distracted enough that I managed to get the door open and slide behind the wheel. My morning coffee may have been broken, but Mo's espresso with an extra shot of anger was working wonders.

He kept hold on the open door and took several calming breaths before he could continue.

"Cyn, I was up all night worrying about you. I went to your apartment and found Winnie passed out on your bed. Carla told me she hadn't heard from you since after dinner and advised me to shove a dildo places I don't personally enjoy dildos... though her phrasing was similar to your recommendation with tampons."

I let out a sigh and shook my head, tugging the door out of his hand.

"We went out to The Ice Box. I think all the missing Canadians are linked to that place based on something Daniel said and the truck James was shoved out of. In the woods behind it, a booby-trapped path with a laser light show led to somewhere but we couldn't get there. Not in the dark, at least. My plan was to check it out after work, but if you want to go out there now go for it. I'm sure you already know where it is."

"What makes you think that?" He asked with a touch of frustration that was ruining my perception of him as the impenetrable Stepford Soldier. Either having sex with me broke him, or he was slowly turning into a real boy from government puppet.

"Doesn't matter."

He chewed on the inside of his cheek, lost in thought before he leaned in and pressed a kiss to my cheek.

"Thanks, chica."

"Yup," I answered, popping the p sound and wondering why I told him. If he was working with the men in the green truck, he probably already knew where it was. If he wasn't... then what? If he didn't find it, he'd think I was lying and if he did... would he make it disappear?

Would it matter as long as he got my missing Canadians home?

I realized I'd been staring at him too long when he stroked a finger along my jaw and I shivered.

"What are you thinking, chica?" His voice was so soft and caring that I almost told him.

Almost.

"Later, Cruz."

He nodded once and I backed out of the alley to spot Larry watching me from his front porch. Larry had a pained look on face turned to horror when Daniel walked out and waved at me before Amber exited behind them with their mother.

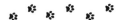

Four hours into my shift, six black sedans pulled up in front of the dairy. Each car spewed two agents in black suits with white shirts and aviator shades. They stepped out in complete synchronicity, and all twelve doors closed at the same time.

After this morning, however, I was ready for the rise of the machines and my inevitable assassination. I'd seen bright lights and heard monster sounds, teamed up with Daniel and watched my ex-boyfriend walk out of a pow wow with his mom and my replacement.

Frankly at this point it would be a blessing to give into the machines and either have my brain placed into a jar or surgically removed and stabbed with electrical probes.

Customers poured out of the dairy, smiling excitedly like they believed this was a flash mob of some sort. All twelve sets of eyes snapped into place, checking every direction with a uniform precision only forced conformity or robotics could master.

Based on the singularity, I was pretty sure that they were robots.

Since I'd seen videos of Nazi soldiers goose-stepping, I reserved a decent margin of error.

"What's going on, Cynthia?" Joseph asked, appearing be-hind me while I crouched low beside a cow who kept shifting uncomfortably. After checking over her legs and the milk-ing equipment, I found that one of her udders had been pinched sideways in the suction tube. I gently tugged it off and checked that she hadn't been injured. The udder was red and raw, but her skin hadn't broken and that meant she wasn't done yet. I swiped the tube with a clean cloth, added a bit of balm to her red and irritated udder before replacing the tube and giving her haunch a gentle scratch.

Personally, I'd have let her have the rest of the day off if I were in charge.

"Best guess? I won't be finishing my shift," I spoke quietly, hoping not to be spotted by the agents who were marching toward the barn two by two. "If you distract them though…"

He stepped out from behind the cow and flagged down the suited collective.

"Can I help you?" Joseph asked and I crab crawled back-ward toward the horse arena.

"We need Cynthia Sharp. Her assistance is requested as part of a national security matter and it can't wait. You will be arrested if you refuse to comply," a short woman with a severe bun provided the robotic dialogue and my stomach dropped into my toes.

I was getting Sarah Connor'ed and if I didn't go willingly, they might hurt the animals.

"I'm right here." Shoving up from the ground, I pulled my-self upright with a wooden crossbeam. "Don't melt metal and murder the livestock with your laser vision and blade arms. I'll go quietly, there's no need to shoot more sheep."

"What are you talking about?" The man beside Lady Robot asked and I noticed how loose his suit was on his thin frame, with ears a bit too big for the rest of his head. "This isn't the Terminator. We legitimately need your help. Though her name is Sarah."

He hooked a thumb toward the woman with the perfect bun.

"And it took twelve of you to ask?" I whistled to Winnie and she bounded out of a stall with a few pieces of straw sticking to the inside of her lips. "Yeah right. Pull out the black sack and get it over with."

"You watch way too many movies," Carla said, shoving her way to the front of the group with Cruz beside her. The pair were the only members of the group in casual attire and I didn't remember seeing them get out of a sedan. "The dairy was on the way to Granny's house and half of these kids were begging for ice cream."

I looked at the suited group and realized only about five had made it into the barn.

"Huh," I shrugged and looked around, spotting a group of agents joking around and shoving each other in the ice cream line. It was like watching a cheerleading team at the mall and part of me questioned if they were really adults. "Alright. We're going to my mom's house?"

"No, we're going to Granny's house," she was fighting the urge to smile. "Granny's Little Shop of Pornos. With speakers to broadcast their pleasure like the shrieking banshees of Transylvania."

"Where is it? Is it near the R. B. Hayes property?" I asked, looking around to make sure the animals were still safe. My eyes stopped on the horses with the word shrieking. Horses were definitely easily startled by shrieking things... Why was that my first thought?

"It's over the river and filled with wood," the first woman, Sarah, cackled. I took a step back when she and Carla high-fived. There was a little too much innuendo being shared over there and I wasn't sure if they were stoned, slap happy or trying too hard to make light of a horror show.

Either way, it looked painfully contagious to smile that much.

Only Cruz had yet to offer a smile, his concern a shadow cast on an otherwise bright moment. While everyone else was relieved to have located the house, Cruz was worried about something more important than finding the house. His appearance had improved in the last four hours, but he still looked weighed down.

"What else?" I asked him and he shook his head in frustration at Carla when she laughed again. "Come on, don't leave me hanging."

Carla and the other woman laughed before sharing another high-five. Cruz rolled his eyes and looked down at his shoes.

"The house is off Braveheart Trail, completely empty and we have no way of knowing where they went. If I'd just gotten there sooner, or looked into it the night of the incident..."

"None of that really seems like your fault... though I admit I'm disappointed," I said, flashing back to Larry's excuse for being tired enough to let Amber have her way with his manbits.

"Disappointed in me?" He looked hurt and I shook my head.

"Disappointed we don't have a Chupacabra."

Chapter Twenty:
Granny's House

"Can you please open a window?" I begged, but the forensic technicians wouldn't allow it.

"Not until they've collected samples from all potential genetic specimens," Carla responded for the second time and I tightened the surgical mask on my face to not breathe in any of the 'genetic material'.

When people talk about cleaning up after a crime scene, most often what I picture is blood. Gallons of blood dried and coating the floor and walls with a bit of excrement from the post-mortem evacuation. Morbid and gross, yes, but I wished I was at one of those scenes instead of this one.

At first glance, the place was clean. There was no blood, just a lingering odor of sweat and muscle ointment. Walking around, the entire cabin had been used for different scenes and I could identify every one of them from the movies my mom had made me watch. The cleanliness of the studio had made me more than willing to walk around and look for any clues as to where they may have taken my missing Canadians.

Until someone turned off the overhead lights and brought out an ultraviolet one.

Everything lit up with splatters and splashes that even the professionals could barely identify. While the directional splatter on the ceiling was quickly identified as semen, there were pools that could have been feminine mucosal secretions... or urine from specialty films I had been lucky enough not to see.

Though the regular lights were back on after the techs had marked where each sample was, I couldn't un-see what they had revealed. We were standing in a petri dish of human secretions and people were drinking coffee and carrying on as though it were nothing.

I'd have felt cleaner in a room with a dead body partially consumed by un-fed pet cats.

"Focus, Cyn," Cruz whispered from my left elbow and I glared at him. "I know how easily distracted you are around hot men and fluid stains, but I'd hate for you to blame me if you get excited."

I fought an eye roll and lost as I jabbed an elbow into his gut.

"First off, eww. Mysterious man juice is so not appetizing. Second, if you saw how excited those old ladies were with those Canadian sausages, your feelings would be hurt because no way have I ever looked at you like that. All that aside, this... is a health hazard. Someone should torch this place and go all scorched earth with it. Knowing how many men and women copulated here is bad enough without seeing the evidence of their off-screen failures," I shuddered at the fluid marker on the top shelf of the linen cabinet. "I'm no forensic scientist, but that looks like someone who got a towel without first washing his hand."

"His hand?" Cruz asked, a smile playing at the corner of his mouth. "I bet a fair amount of that sausage juice was on the hands of the women 'copulating' them."

"Gross, Cruz. Just gross. I know you missed the porn screening, but those little old ladies are short. Like... my mom and Mrs. Margot short. If they were the ones getting something from the top shelf, there'd be smears on every shelf below it and a step stool. Except not, because they'd have rinsed the gunk off their hands before getting the towel."

The nearest forensic tech considered me for a moment, a scowl forming on his face.

"No offense?" I told him, unsure if he was upset by my criticism of short people or the cleanliness of men.

"So... what does all this," he gestured wide. "Say to you?"

"That if these men weren't enjoying their indentured servitude, however illegal, there wouldn't have been so much on-camera smiling or gratuitous fluid stains. Since I've seen the films, I can also tell you that no semen actually hit the ceiling on camera. Which means that was either a for-fun ejaculation or he messed up and released too soon. It's not like these guys are professionals, they can only orgasm when stimulated and aroused. I'm aware that the body reacts to stimulation with or without the owner's consent, but look at that wall," I gestured toward a pair of markers that showed a splatter pattern at least eight inches long. "If the penis was being forced to ejaculate, the manipulator would control where the semen goes. You know who gets ejaculate everywhere? Men having a good time."

A female crime tech held out her hand and I gave her a fist bump.

"Think this is what your bathroom looked like yesterday after we..." I slapped my hand over his mouth to stop him from talking.

"Whatever fun and games happened in the privacy of my shower are not relevant at this moment," I hissed and he laughed beneath my palm, pressing a kiss against it. I pulled my hand back and wiped it on my pants.

"Are you saying all of this was just fun and games?" He asked and my eyes searched the floor and counters for any other line of inquiry or investigative leads. In the regular light, the space looked clean and empty. Despite the obvious signs of activity marked on the walls, floor, and ceiling, something was missing.

What should be in here?

I started in the kitchen and listed the first things that came to mind.

"Food, garbage, soap..." I moved between techs and looked into the hall bathroom. "Toilet paper, hand towels, cleaning products."

"What about them?" He asked, watching me search every bathroom and bedroom until I had a complete picture.

"No one lived at this house," I stated, opening closets to see dust covered shelves and plastic wrapped dry cleaning on hangers. "This house was just for filming... but..."

I avoided a few more evidence markers to look out the window. Around the house was a dirt buffer that would serve as a parking lot, but there weren't many tire treads overlapping. When a large group of cars gathered, tracks became less distinct but I could easily make out three distinct groups disappearing around the corner.

I walked to the bedroom across the hall. Outside this bedroom was softer dirt, closer to mud. A single pattern of tires went through it, but there were footprints beside the tracks and it went the same direction as the treads on the other side of the house. I pressed my face to the glass, trying to see where they went when Cruz pulled my face away from the window.

"Don't do that, chica," he warned, and I blinked at him in confusion.

"Do what?" I asked, looking between him and the window.

"Put your face on anything in this house," he chuckled, and I gagged.

"Oh my dog!" I ran into the bathroom and turned on the tap, ripping off my surgical mask. Without waiting for it to warm up, I splashed it on my face, scrubbing with my fingers and plastering hair to my face in an effort to feel clean. "Why did you let me do that?!?"

The bastard just stood in the doorway, laughing.

"I don't *let* you do anything, chica. You make poor choices all on your own."

"Laugh all you want, I will have my revenge!" I shouted at him and he smirked.

"I didn't do anything. It's your face."

I stuck my tongue out at him like the grown woman I was and he leaned in to capture it with his lips. A juvenile act turned into a kiss that sent tingles all over my body, he gripped my arms and placed them around his neck before gripping my hips and pulling me closer.

His hand grazed my arm and every part of me caught fire as I tried desperately to get him closer, knowing full well no good could come from our time together.

"I'm sorry," he whispered against my mouth and I pulled away. I searched his face and the area around us, trying to figure out what he was apologizing for. If it were anyone else, I'd have said no way could he read my mind, but he'd been eerily close to repeating my thoughts verbatim more than once. "I will always protect you, and the people you love. Just... don't give up on me."

His soft words pulled on my heart strings and I gave a single nod in his direction.

I also thought the word cheese loudly to see if he would bring me some, but it didn't work.

It was probably a selective mind reading ability. Like Winnie's listening skills in the presence of something edible. Like cheese... or Ian Cruz.

That last one was definitely a personal weakness.

"Now that your face is clean... kind of. Should we see if we can figure out where those footprints go or do you want to add to the black light splatters?" He winked and squeezed my hip suggestively.

My face flamed, and I pushed him away from me. The mind reading power was back and I had to get out of here before he figured out I wanted to eat him and contaminate a crime scene.

"I- uh..." I moved around him out of the bathroom and made a beeline for the front door. Cruz followed quietly and I tried to avoid eye contact with everyone we passed on our way out. They did not extend the same courtesy and more than one wolf whistle came our way.

You kissed Cruz surrounded by the jizz of strangers, my brain reminded me. I gave up my dignity to run out of the house and straight to my Jeep as a smattering of snickers followed me out of the door.

"Do I want to know what you're thinking?" Ian's eyes were laughing but his mouth was in a position that begged me to kiss it again. Maybe even take a nibble and then his shirt could be disposed of...

"Nope. Definitely not," I spun around, tapped on the window of my Jeep, trying to calm my irrational body. I woke Sleeping Beauty and waited for her to look at me. "You ready girl?"

She stretched and leapt onto the ground beside me as soon as I opened the door.

Winnie and Cruz followed me to the side of the cabin and I looked closely at the footprints in the damp dirt. There were at least four different pairings, but it was impossible to tell if they were one man wearing different shoes or several walking the same path repeatedly. Cruz focused his attention on the tire track and Winnie pranced to the tree line for a bathroom break.

"What are your thoughts?" I asked Cruz, and he shrugged.

"I'm not really a car guy, but if I had to guess I'd say they belonged to a truck," I nodded at his response and waited for Winnie to finish making a puddle that rivaled the Great Lakes. "What are your thoughts on the shoes?"

He was crouching beside me, studying the indentations and I compared his feet and mine to the impressions.

"Tall, probably work boots, and going that way," I inclined my head toward the rear of the property as Winnie trotted up beside us. "One or four people walking at a time, and definitely more than once on either count."

My dog led the way, sniffing the ground and picking up speed as the scent got stronger. We pushed our speed and followed her between two trees to a tool shed.

"If that's filled with hanging chainsaws and a masked man in a jumpsuit," I paused, taking a step back while Cruz pointed to the doorknob. Winnie sniffed and sat in confirmation before he turned the handle and opened it. He swept the wooden box with his flashlight, before Winnie nudged him aside and went in. We followed her to the back corner and waited for her to sniff thoroughly. Instead, she went directly to the back wall and sat again. A gust of air came out of the wall, and then it was gone.

"Seriously?" I whispered, moving forward and pulling out a flashlight of my own.

We were at the entrance to an earth tunnel that had been dug out and outfitted with support beams. Inside it, there were clearly four large sets of footprints and two smaller ones. Cautiously, I sniffed inside the tunnel and Winnie copied me, offering a head tilt in response.

"What are you looking for?" Cruz asked, going into the tunnel first and letting Winnie and I follow.

"Whatever kills canaries in coal mines," I whispered and he looked back at me with an expression that I couldn't read in the dark. If I had to guess, I had amused him in some way.

"We aren't mining, how would the carbon monoxide get here?"

Winnie and I shared a look.

"Does it matter? I'd rather check and not find it than die suddenly," I grumbled and Cruz pulled me forward to press a kiss to my lips. "What was that for?"

"Being you," he said, letting me go so we could continue through the tunnel. It was cooler down here, the air held a fresh scent that mingled with the dirt and damp wood framing the tunnel. If I had to put a name to it...

"Do you smell dryer sheets?" I asked and Cruz stopped to sniff for a moment. On instinct, I checked my pockets and came up with snake eyes.

"Yeah." He moved to the walls and shined his flashlight, but there was nothing there. "What do you think..."

I stuffed my hands into his pockets and felt something that was decidedly not a dryer sheet. Accepting the invitation, he pulled me backwards by my pant loops, back searching for the tunnel's edge to get a better purchase.

We ran into a wall and he let out a huff of air when he narrowly avoided smashing the back of his head into it. Releasing my belt loops with a disappointed sigh, we got back to work. Taking opposite ends of the assumed opening, we pressed softly along the edge, trying to see if there was a handle, hinges or air flow moving from the other side.

I slipped on a muddy patch and threw my hand out to stop from falling flat on my face. The wall turned out to be a door that shifted and light crept into the tunnel. A strong whiff of clean laundry came through with a gust of hot air and I stopped Cruz from charging in to listen. There were voices on the other side.

"Ruined all the fun," one of them said and the other snorted in agreement.

"Now how will we pass the time? I'm not really interested in going back to self-service, even if the upkeep was easier." At the sound of the second woman, Winnie shoved her way through the door and entered the room. "Oh, hello Winnie."

Confused, I followed my dog and found myself in a basement laundry room with Mrs. Margot and one of the women I'd seen on film. She was easily recognized by her ace of spades tattoo and one fake eye that only faced forward.

"Cynthia, Ian... are you here to arrest us?" She asked and we shared a look.

"For what?" He managed to get it out first and I waited for the answer hoping she didn't have Cruella aspirations for my best friend.

"Tricking those men into acting in our films and keeping them from their families," she said seriously. "We weren't interested in making money, but that man sort of convinced us it would be worth it and I've always wanted to act."

"You... I'm sorry. What?" I asked and she rubbed Winnie's head affectionately.

"Oh dear. I can see she's started to take after that Kirby boy," the woman beside Mrs. Margot said and both women snickered. "Perhaps we should dumb it down for her."

Another cackle was shared between the two and I felt Cruz suppressing his own behind me.

"We smuggled those men into this country for consensual sex, but now they've been abducted. Since we didn't bring them here properly, we're technically human traffickers and possibly accessories to their abduction since we hardly tried to stop the men taking them away."

"What men?" I asked, wondering why they'd let their sex toys go so easily.

"Short pudgy man and a tall one, a bit weaselly looking. Noah and John, bless their hearts, were far more trouble to keep then they were worth. Ate us out of house and home and couldn't keep their bathroom clean to a basic human standard. Urine everywhere, just like their baby batter."

I gagged at her use of the term "baby batter" and said a silent plea to the gods of werewolf smut that that never appeared in my books again.

Instant buzzkill.

"These men, did you see them get here? What were they driving?"

"Of course we saw them, do you think we would just give those boys to anyone? We made sure they had ample snacks and even cleaned them some underwear for the trip. Loaded everything into a green pick-up and kissed them goodbye. The men said they needed the boys for arranging an agreement and promised the men it wouldn't hurt them. Strangest thing though, instead of driving toward town, they went the other way. Not much out there besides that old abandoned president's mansion where they had that explosion the other night."

Chapter Twenty-One: Drive-by Mail

C ruz and I drove home in absolute silence.

There were no words to explain the day we had just survived and trying to find those words had given me a migraine. A late night of running through the woods followed by an early morning of tending to livestock had been bad enough, but that wasn't the extent of my punishment for being a failure at life.

Robotic suit people invading the dairy had nearly faded from my memory at this point, and the sun still hadn't had the decency to set. Thinking the machines had come for me was not the weirdest part of my day, but it held the distinguished spot of most stressful. Neither was witnessing the set of a porn film light up like New Year's Eve in New York under a black light. Add in a secret tunnel to a certified man cave and images of both would likely grace my nightmares for weeks to come. I can officially add buried alive in a box full of trash and semen to my growing list of "Ways I Do Not Want to Die" and "Ways of Dying I Never Previously Thought Possible".

Sadly it was not the first thing to make both lists, but it was definitely ranked higher. Unlike the rest of the lists, no one had died buried in semen, garbage and dirt. The entire idea was a compilation of too many horrific scenes for my mind to process individually.

Which meant if anyone could manage to die being buried alive and covered in semen and garbage, it was me.

After the laundry room confession, Cruz had called the people back at the other house and a team arrived to secure everything for the initial sweep. Once we looked at the whole house, I understood why the men's locker room was off limits in every gym, barracks and war zone I had been in. It wasn't a public decency thing like we thought.

It wasn't even an anti-harassment issue.

Bachelor men of all ages were just outright disgusting and I now firmly believe that the hole in the ground employee restroom at The Ice Box was actually a voted on and approved choice.

There were three floors of horror, not counting the laundry room where we found Mrs. Margot. The dorm style rooms they occupied in the upper floors of the laundry house were filled

to the brim with dirty clothes, moldy food and dirty maga-
zines that made what they did on film look tame. Mrs. Margot
and Ms. Skinner, also known as Ruby and Pearl, had required
the men shower before hooking up, both on and off camera.
Other than that, though, they'd left them responsible for
their own cleanliness and hygiene.

Which meant they neglected everything but the bare minimum to be sexually acceptable.

To top it off, not only had we witnessed two old ladies
arrested for immigration fraud and human trafficking, but
Mrs. Margot popped out her teeth and offered the agent a
"blowie" if he'd give her that one phone call now.

After she made that phone call, sans "blowie" as far as we
were aware, suddenly every record of their actions had van-
ished. Every Canadian was legal and had a permit to work in
this country. That permit also included provisions allowing
them to work and receive payment in the sex performance
industry.

Hiring paperwork was on file with a registered LLC, that
operated as a film studio with private financier backing. Mrs.
Margot had conveniently forgotten she owned both the LLC
and the hedge fund that sponsored it.

While I suspected Mrs. Margot had called her niece "the
cracker", I couldn't bring myself to throw either woman under
the bus. The paperwork may not have been in order from the
beginning, but the men agreed to come here exclusively to perform explicit acts with older women. In exchange for the visa,
the women had only asked for partners willing to live with them

until their estrogen supplements leveled off and they were "less horny".

The films were added after the fact as blackmail.

Now the blackmailer had the Canadians, but now that they were citizens I wasn't sure how they could be leveraged.

Carla had taken a small team to look at the R. B. Hayes Estate. Neither Cruz nor I was clear on how the Sweet Pea Chief of Police had authority over a government property, but somehow, she was the point person to this whole operation and the only one who was allowed to know everything going on in an otherwise compartmentalized mission. For once, it wasn't Cruz keeping secrets, he was just as upset at being kept in the dark as I was.

Whatever she found there had yet to be shared with us and I was grateful for the reprieve.

"Where are we?" I asked, looking out of the passenger side window. Cruz and I had ended up driving back in one of the many black sedans with no clue who owned it. The government, much like the fictional Rangeman organization, never seemed to run out of black cars and men to drive them. "I thought we were going to the dairy so I could get my Jeep back."

"That was one suggestion, but I decided to go another route," he answered, putting the car in park. We were in front of a small farmhouse, painted white with wooden railing and fenced off to the rear. "That other route being you stay here... with me."

My lower body stood at attention and purred.

"Another safe house?" I asked, remembering the last time he took me somewhere for the night. I woke up hungover in an apartment that looked more like a bomb shelter than a place where people live as non-vampiric persons. What sat in front of us looked like a place someone might actually live.

"Not exactly," he answered, climbing out of the car. I followed him out, letting Winnie run free as I studied the ranch home. It was one story with a wraparound porch, and I marveled at the bay window box and the chimney that promised a cozy fireplace in the winter.

"It's perfect," I said quietly, moving toward the road so I could see where we were. Maybe if I saved a governor I could demand this house in exchange for my services. A large shrub obstructed most of the front of the house from the road and I had to walk all the way to the end of the gravel drive to see an address.

Except instead of an address, there was a wooden sign hanging on two eye hooks squeaking at the end of a gold chain.

Professional Dog Training and Boarding

Ian Cruz, Army K-9 Trainer

Retired

Footsteps crunched up the driveway and I looked at Cruz. His feet shuffled nervously as his hand reached down to pet Winnie. She sat on his foot and leaned against his leg, offering him a lolling tongue of affectionate approval.

"You... retired?" I asked, looking between him, the sign and Winnie. "You're... staying... here?"

I read the address and found we were only about four miles away from the dairy.

"What? How?" He just shrugged his shoulders and gave me a small smile.

"Want to see inside?"

The smile turned suggestive and I felt one of my own in response.

"Sure. How many beds are there?" I offered him a quizzical look and his suggestive smile went outright filthy.

"Three... and they are in dire need of quality control before the thirty-day in-home warranty expires," he answered, taking my hand and pulling me flush against him before kissing me so hard I forgot how to breathe. "If you're really good, I'll let you try them all twice."

Oh boy.

The house was perfect.

In addition to the beautiful aesthetic, he'd filled it with three coffee makers, cheese crackers and chocolate chip cookies. Everything was rustic but cleaned up in a fresh coat of paint with modern appliances and high-speed internet.

Well, almost perfect.

"Who bought your coffee cups? Lilliputians?" I asked, holding up a generic white coffee cup that looked like something hotels put in their rooms to discourage thievery and proper caffeination.

"Cabinet above the coffee maker," he said, taking the micro-mug from my hand and hanging it back beside its friends. I scowled at him for stealing my mug but obliged his request and opened the cupboard.

Now the house was perfect.

"Did you... are these... for me?" I asked, looking between him and the 16oz mugs with dog silhouettes and snarky sayings. Half of them were near duplicates of ones I had at my own house, from the Jurassic Dog Park to my personal favorite, a unicorn giving everyone the finger.

"If I say yes, do I get a prize?" He took a step forward and reached for my hip, digging his fingers into the tender muscles until I let out a gasp of pleasure that was only tarnished by my body's lack of coffee.

"I don't put out before coffee, bub." I scoffed, pouring a hefty amount in a mug. It declared the drinker was "Working toward Working Dog Level" with a psychotic looking malinois on it. I added a half gallon of coffee creamer to it for posterity and joy. "Try again later and do it with chocolate."

"You are such an easy woman to please," he groped my chest and headed into the living room.

"When did you buy all of this?" I asked, following him and sitting on a couch that was far more comfortable than it looked. "Have you told the Army you're retiring? Because they don't act like they know you're retiring or that they'd let you."

"I didn't... not exactly. It's..." but I didn't get to find out the rest of his sentence before a brick shattered the bay window at the front of the house. We ran to the front in time to see a green pick-up truck fishtailing its way up the gravel road and squealing off down the road in a cloud of dust.

"Are you OK?" I asked Cruz, listening for a grunt of confirmation.

My eyes took in the damage while my hands sought Winnie. She was safely behind me when I reached for my cell phone and snapped a picture to send to Carla before scrambling around to keep Winnie away from the broken glass. I sat her on the couch, grabbing some slippers I saw in a hall closet and sliding them on my feet before grabbing a second pair for Cruz.

Except he was already wearing shoes.

I studied him, looking from his face to his hands. The light cast shadows through the broken window, hiding his face, but it couldn't conceal the truth. Despite the damage to his house, Cruz remained calm, indifferent.

Like he was expecting this, I realized and he looked at me with a nod.

"It's another safe house," he confirmed, gesturing for me to pick up the brick with the note attached. "Except it wasn't supposed to be."

"What was it supposed to be?" I asked, unfolding the note and examining the vague and ominous message.

Trade us for the men, or everyone dies.

You know where to meet us for the trade.

This secret will remain buried.

"It was supposed to be mine," he sighed, looking at the broken glass. "It was supposed to be mine and like everything else, the government asked me to give it up for something they thought was more important. Except this time... this time I agreed with them. The price was worth it, but I thought I'd have more time."

"So, your name was on the front as a lure? This was another baited hook?" I asked, reading the letter again. "What do they want you to trade them for? What was important enough to let them use your future home?"

His eyes met mine and I knew even before he spoke what the answer would be.

"They want you... and Winnie."

Chapter Twenty-Two: Evidentiary Support

"Where is the trade-off location?" I asked Carla, knowing that she was more likely to tell me than Cruz. "Is it the Estate?"

"No. The Estate was just the place for the party. The government has a lot of properties here. All of them have their own histories and unique features that make them ideal spots for a prisoner hand-off and we'd normally look into all of them to be certain which location they were interested in. In this case, we don't need to research. The target has expressed interest in one specific property before and the team observing it has noticed an influx of cars and activity but have yet to positively identify any of the major players we're looking for," her response sounded like a press release, but it was more information than what I had before.

None of it was particularly helpful at the moment, but I filed it away for later.

"Is the property nearby?" I asked and she gave a curt nod. "And this is about justice for Africa? Or is it about something else?"

Carla paused for a long moment, and I didn't think she would answer. If Conri Kade had been placed in protection to testify against his now missing father who worked with the government to commit mass murder, was the target Conri's dad or was someone threatening to expose everything?

"Have you seen the movie *Charlie Wilson's War*?" She kept her eyes on the road and I watched as we passed the dairy so I could grab clean clothes from my apartment. She promised to drive me back to the dairy for my shift afterward, but I noticed Cruz checking my pockets attempting to locate the keys to my Jeep.

Joke was on him, though. I'd hidden my keys at the dairy when I thought the robots had come for me so they couldn't get my cheese sandwich crackers.

On me too, because I hid them in Joseph's pocket and his alcoholic behaviors meant his pants could be anywhere. Based on past experience with drunk Joseph, *anywhere* was at least limited to his house, office and the rear quarter acre where he yelled at corn and sunflowers for being yellow.

The man hated the color yellow.

"Is that the Tom Hanks movie where all the government officials snort cocaine with strippers and trade favors to get what they want?" I answered her. "And America was letting the Soviets commit genocide in the Middle East just to watch them spin their wheels like the Americans had confronting them... somewhere? There is a black hole fund that he used to train and arm the citizens but then failed to follow through with essential infrastructure. The decision is ultimately what caused the 9/11 attack though I don't think that was in the movie."

Carla nodded and turned onto Main Street.

"One of the hardest resources to manage is human behavior. We can know what to do, but it's a lot harder to get everyone to agree to do more than what is considered the bare minimum for survival. It's easy to take a life, we both know that, but it's a lot harder to put down the weapons and re-build afterward. There's always that fear that if we give too much, the people we are trying to help will get too powerful and use those same tools we gave them to destroy us."

"So, the villages that were destroyed, were those people killed because they were a threat or were they allies until someone else came in? What tools did we give them?"

"In this instance, neither. The location was a resource we failed to protect, and the outcome was a choice of their death or ours. At the time of the bombing, only the insurgents and infected were in the village. Though I have yet to find someone who can tell me what organization went in or how Conri's dad came into play... or even Conri himself. It would seem this one is extremely tight lipped, but I know the basics. Have you seen the movie *Outbreak*?" She asked and I tilted my head, trying to think back. I'd read a lot of Richard Preston books, including *The Hot Zone* and *Cobra Event*. If memory serves, the movie *Outbreak* was based on *The Hot Zone* with one caveat.

"The government was creating biological weapons in Africa, but someone made a mistake and the virus ended up in America..." The wheels in my head started turning and I stared at Carla.

"Are you saying that the American government was making biological weapons in Africa and blew up four African villages to cover it up when an opposing force discovered the secret and tried to steal it? Did they bomb the villages because the virus got out, or did they blow them up to keep other people from having their weapon? How can they be sure no innocent people were still in the villages?" I was suddenly very upset with my heritage and service history. We were as bad as the British in the 1700s. "When did this happen?"

"The short answer, we can't prove there wasn't collateral damage and I can't be sure if the bombing was to stop the virus from getting out or stop the people who supposedly invaded from telling the world. George Bush, senior, was president at the time, so it must have been the early 1990s. I don't know if he was involved in the weapons themselves or only cleaning up after the fact. Cruz told you Ohio has been the birthplace of eight past presidents, the last was in the 1920s during prohibition. Though he was a republican and the president at the time, Taft opposed the amendment even as he enforced it. We think the choice of locations in this area is symbolic, but it's just speculation. This state has a long and notable history, but it hasn't been as prominent in recent years. If you want to lay low and take advantage of history, Ohio's a good place to start."

She pulled up outside my building and parked on the curb.

"Head on up and change, I'll wait here," she said, and I nodded, but didn't exit as my mind tried to make connections.

Prohibition was the government's solution to a perceived weakness in its population. Alcohol had been treated as the catch-all source of the nation's problems and banning it only served to strengthen the criminal activity they sought to prevent.

Evidence was hard to come by. Alcohol was moved underground in tunnels, but it was also widely approved of by the general public. If no one was willing to confess or turn over physical proof, it was a game of whack-a-mole where you tried to grab the distributors before they could disappear back underground.

"Cyn?" Carla said and I shook off my trance.

"Right, sorry." I climbed out of the car and let Winnie out of the back seat. She stretched and yawned before prancing beside me to the front door. Together, we unlocked the front door to my office, re-locked it, and trooped upstairs to my apartment.

Everything was where I had left it, with one addition.

"Why are you on my couch?" I asked Joel, surprised to see him outside of the R. B. Hayes estate and without a notebook. The suit he sported was clean and pressed, a good indication he'd changed since the morning after the attack.

"Are you alone?"

I growled at having my question answered with a question and Winnie showed him her teeth. Instead of looking concerned, he rolled his eyes at both of us.

"It's a simple question, Ms. Sharp. Why are you so irritable? Are you alone?"

Winnie kept her gaze locked on the man, working her way to the bed in the corner. She leapt up and laid down, facing him in sphinx pose.

"I'm never alone. Answer my question."

He kept his eyes on Winnie for another moment and I watched the gears in his head turning. Was he here to take Winnie? I casually moved into the kitchen and opened my coffee cup cabinet, taking down a mug and looping my fingers through the prong taser at the same time. Setting the taser down without revealing it from behind the mug, I dropped a kitchen towel on top of it. When Joel continued to watch Winnie, I exhaled slowly before placing the mug in the single-serve machine with a coffee pod.

His eyes darted back to me when the coffee maker rattled the counter.

"I'm here to get your help. Mr. Kade is deeply concerned about who is trustworthy. I have been thoroughly vetted and you have proven yourself to be competent, intelligent and resourceful. We are asking you to trust us in return by coming with me."

"Going with you where?" I asked, pulling out a creamer container and a spoon as the coffee maker chugged. Aside from the taser, I wasn't near any other weapons. It would be better to play along than risk mine or Winnie's safety.

"Mr. Kade has been relocated to another estate. He is asking you to meet him at a neighboring property with Sgt. Pupperson to see if it is a suitable place for him to lay low until the threat has been neutralized." Joel tapped his fingers on the coffee table and I searched for a pattern in the movement.

"The threat being... his father who attacked the villages?" The tapping sped up, more fervent and erratic.

"Yes. That threat," he answered, but I saw sweat on his forehead. Interesting... his nervousness indicated he knew something different than what Carla knew, but not necessarily more.

"Well, Carla is outside. I'll ride with her and we'll follow you to this estate. She can verify its security features and suitability. Then we'll make sure the government knows where you and Mr. Kade are. For safety reasons," I challenged his intention and was satisfied to see him shift in his seat. "Carla is waiting for me, she won't leave until I come back down. Perhaps I should text her?"

"No! That wouldn't be wise. She hasn't been vetted!" He pulled out a phone and worked the keys. "I'll just let her know that you and Winnie have been called in to perform a service."

Liar, liar, ants in your pants fire.

Winnie wagged her tail, and we shared a look before I went back to looking at Joel.

Who was now pointing a gun at me.

"We're running low on time. Give me your cell phone, grab your dog and follow me out quietly," he ordered and I let out a soft whistle. Winnie jumped toward him, sinking her teeth into his forearm while I grabbed the taser.

"Winnie, out," I commanded, and she released his arm while he howled in pain. Seizing the moment, I deployed the taser and watched his body twitch with the electrical jolt. A wet spot appeared on his pants and before I could feel appalled at having to clean it up, a sharp stick poked my neck just as a red feather-topped pen landed in Winnie.

"Winnie!" I started, but my eyes were losing focus and the room swam above me. "Winnie!"

A man appeared above me with slicked back hair and a pointy face.

"Alec Alan Glen?" I slurred and he shook his head.

"Jared." His sneer reminded me that he'd been at the table with Joel and Mr. Kade. I was also completely off with his name, but not his weaselly face. "If you want your Canadians back and to come out of this alive, keep your voice down."

"All of you are betraying him. Need to help..."

My eyes started to drift closed as two large men appeared. One went straight to Winnie, picking her up while the other grabbed me like a sack of potatoes.

Chapter Twenty-Three: Inconvenient Incarceration

The gentle rumble of a diesel engine was my first clue things weren't going well for me. My second clue was the sharp metal pole digging into my ribcage and the absence of light to see either the truck or the pole.

Given that I had been in my non-moving apartment in near broad daylight, engines and darkness were definitely not good.

"Winnie?" I whispered, but nothing moved nearby. "Winnie?"

My arms were tingling with circulation loss and I wiggled them around to get feeling back. It was odd that my arms had stayed trapped underneath me, but I couldn't get anywhere until I woke them back up. A decision I regretted when the sharp metal cuffs dug into my wrists and the pins and needles were joined by the sting of uneven metal cutting into my skin.

Arms handcuffed behind back, not ideal.

Biting down hard, I fought against the scream and wiggled sideways to see if the rod on my back could help with the cuffs. Something slid away as the vehicle slowed down and clattered around the area by my feet. Whatever the metal rod had been, I couldn't get to it now.

The floor was metal, my body laid flat and straight along a ridged surface that rumbled with the engine. The air inside was stagnant and warm, like the inside of an oven. Squirming further, I ran into a hump the length of my back.

Wheel well, I'm in the bed of a truck. After a mental pat on the back, I realized something more pressing. *Why the hell is it so dark?*

Kicking out my right, I felt a pinch on my ankle that bit into my left one.

Leg cuffs, great.

Lifting both legs, my toes crashed into something rigid. I scooted over and kicked again, same result.

Truck lid?

It would explain both the heat and the trapped air. Sweat was pooling under my arms and the cuffs were getting slippery, though they refused to give.

Worming my way the other direction, my shoulder ran into something solid and warm. Flopping to the side, I reached my hands out to poke it. When nothing happened, I ran my hands back and forth, trying to force my hands to feel everything.

It was soft... fluffy...

"Winnie!" I shouted and then clenched my mouth shut hoping no one had heard me. The engine's rumble continued and I exhaled slowly. My hands pressed hard against her soft side and I held my breath. "Where is it... come on..."

My fingertips glided up and down her back as the first tear pooled in the corner of my eye.

"Please no..."

Everything else disappeared beyond the tips of my fingers. My own heart thundering in my ears as I tried to find her pulse, pressing into every part of her my fingers were touching. I probed and squeezed before...

Pooft.

The air moved beside my hand and I realized my error just before I gagged.

It wasn't her back, I had been pressing on her tail.

Fighting back the urge to throw up, I moved the other direction with my hands, past her furry butt and up her back to the squishy belly that had never once met a snack it didn't like. My hand traced that to just beneath her rib cage, before I pressed down and tried to slow my own panic to feel for a sign of life beyond flatulence.

She was breathing and her heart rate was steady.

"Oh thank dog," I whispered before another *pooft* escaped and I choked. The sweat coating my hands collected her fur and no amount of wiggling could eliminate the uncomfortable itch of sweaty fur. When she let out a third fart, I gave up and laid back, waiting for the nightmare to end.

"No more tranquilizers for us, yeah?" I asked, blaming them for her gas and the throb between my eyes. "Also no more seatbelt-less car rides. This isn't safe."

My point was reinforced almost immediately.

Everything shifted left and the smooth ride ended. The truck started careening from side to side like the cars on the Indiana Jones ride. Winnie and I were thrown against each other, the lid and the ground as we bumped along what could only be a dirt road. Bending my feet behind me, I squirmed closer to Winnie. Once I was flush against her, I nudged us both until I touched the wall of the truck bed and braced her body between us to prevent injury. If she was unconscious, she wouldn't be able to protect herself from the impact and I fought my own self-preservation instinct to protect her. My shoulder slammed repeatedly into the hard metal as I fought to keep Winnie steady with my body, legs cramping as my sweat formed a slippery slide that stole my traction.

Still, I fought inertia until the truck hit a deep rut, my head slammed down into the truck bed and I was out.

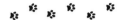

"Take them inside, you idiots! This wasn't the plan!" A man was shouting and something sticky coated the side of my face. Bright sunlight invaded my eyelids before I was floating through the air on the shoulder of a man.

"They're still breathing," the man beneath me rumbled and I tried to hold still. Whatever they needed us for, I did not want to appear awake enough to find out until Winnie was able to run with me.

"She has blood on her face and the dog could have been injured! What happens if you broke her nose? I'm running out of time!"

Angry man sounded familiar, his voice disappearing when we left the bright sun and stepped into a cool dark interior. We went up fifteen steps before I was tossed roughly on a springy bed and something warm and heavy was placed on top of me. My focus went to my breathing, forcing it to be deep and even while fighting the urge to open my eyes and study the surroundings.

"Think we should wipe off the blood?" One of the men asked and the air shifted as one leaned over and breathed salmon and garlic onto my face.

"Nah, waste of time. She just needs to hold the leash. As soon as they find the device they're dead anyway."

The door opened, closed and a lock clicked into place. Counting to ten, I listened carefully for any other breathing or signs of life in the room.

Hearing nothing, I sat up and opened my eyes.

Everything about this room reminded me of visiting the R. B. Hayes estate. The furniture and decoration was from another time, and a fine layer of dust said that that time was before the invention of Pledge and dust rags.

Winnie was draped across my lap, breathing steadily and keeping my shins nice and toasty. I leaned my face in to sniff her fur, curious what newborn mothers were going on about, when I saw her collar.

The idiots had left her collar on.

Scooting backward, I bent my legs against my chest and moved my arms along my butt to my sit bones. Kicking off my work boots, I pointed my toes and slipped one foot at a time to the other side of the cuffs. It was a tight squeeze, but I got my arms up the front of my legs and cuffed in front of my body.

"OK," I whispered, waiting for my abdominal cramp to pass before reaching for the pink camo collar and checking the D-ring on the front. Looped to it was a key to my apartment and a handcuff key I'd added last month after an experimentation with bondage gone awry.

Carefully, I pried the key loop apart with my thumbnail and worked the handcuff key in a circle until it came loose at the end. I lifted the key to my mouth and positioned it between my teeth, aiming it for the key hole on the cuffs and shoving it in. Pulling my face away, I twisted my wrists in, grabbed hold of the key and turned.

The cuffs popped loose and I threw them to the floor, not anticipating the loud thud that would come with it.

"Crap, crap, crap," I whispered, stuffing the key in my ankle shackles and trying to listen for footsteps on the stairs. The second set of shackles popped off and I held my breath with my feet and hands pressed together when the doorknob wiggled.

A voice murmured on the other side and the knob wiggled some more before someone below us shouted and footsteps moved away from the door. Sliding my boots back on, I stood up and searched the room quickly, finding nothing to use as a weapon.

The room had a connected bathroom and I carefully put some water in my hands before taking a small sip. Refilling the divot of one hand, I carried it to Winnie's face and pressed the liquid against her nose. It twitched once, twice, and then her pink tongue snaked out and dipped into the water.

"Good girl," I whispered, getting her more water. After a second drink, she jumped to the floor and shook, collar jingling and floor shaking. "Crap! No Shhh..."

It was too late.

Several sets of shoes ran to the door and the lock popped open to reveal Conri, Jared the weasel man, and...

"Terminator Lady? You need to get Conri out of here. Weasel man is with the bad guys..." her eyes remained blank and it clicked into place. Who else would have put a gun in the kitchen besides the man paying for the event. "You're all working together? What the heck? Are you even hiding from your dad?"

She smiled and Conri mirrored the slightly maniacal and creepy expression. All three produced flat black semi-automatic handguns and I sighed at the improbability of escaping that many bullets.

"No, Ms. Sharp. My father was framed to take the heat off of them, but now I need leverage so I can finally rid myself of your government's boot on my neck."

Winnie let out a soft whimper and I got the impression she regretted protecting him the night of his fundraising party. With a look, I promised her he wouldn't get away with it, but that was overly optimistic.

"Since you're both awake now, let's get this over with."

Chapter
Twenty-Four:
Tunnel Vision

W innie's first instinct was to protect me, but I signaled for her to stand down. She grumbled and huffed but chose to listen... this time. We were both stubborn and reckless, but neither of us would risk the other getting hurt, not until we were out of options.

Or came across some snacks.

In this case, I was just hoping to learn why we were going to die before it actually happened.

Jared took the lead, Conri gesturing for me to follow Jared before he and Sarah took up the rear. At the bottom of the stairs,

I started toward the door while Jared turned the corner. A gun shoved into my kidney elicited a low growl from Winnie.

"Muzzle that beast," Sarah snapped, her eyes locked on Winnie and I sensed her fear. Sarah was either afraid of dogs or disliked them, both of which made her even more of a terrible person than she already was. I made a mental note to use Winnie against her when possible.

Sure, maybe we wouldn't survive, but at least these three were going with us.

More if I could manage it.

I turned to look at Conri as Jared led us toward the kitchen and out onto a sun deck. Since I came in unconscious, I didn't know where we were in relation to the truck that brought us here, but the area looked similar to the Hayes Estate. Off the beaten path and concealed by trees and farmland.

"Do you have a muzzle?"

"What the hell would I have a muzzle for?" Sarah countered with an annoyed look in her eyes. "It's not like I have a dog."

"No, but he does," I smirked toward Conri. "And I assume that dog sometimes has trouble keeping her mouth shut. Kind of like right now."

Her gun came down on my cheek and I tasted blood.

"Look here you dumb-"

"Enough Sarah," Conri scolded her with a smile playing on his lips. "You are even, now. No one hits my guests without my permission. Your one warning."

"Yes sir," she looked down at her shoes and I waited for her to talk back. Instead, the woman remained silent, walking demurely beside him until I bumped into Jared's back and faltered. Startled, I looked between her, Jared and Mr. Kade.

"What was that?" I asked, trying to keep up with Jared as he exited onto the lawn. The bright sun was burning my retinas, but I followed toward a rear building that was probably a carriage house converted into servants' quarters or something else equally antiquated and insulting. If this man had forced a Federal Agent into subserviency, I didn't want to know what else he did in his free time.

Which naturally meant I asked anyway.

"Are you some kind of Dom?" He met my gaze and held it, daring me to say more.

"You will find, Ms. Sharp, that I enjoy control. Being held all these years as both bait and prisoner was taxing, but not without its merits. One of those merits is Sarah, who takes great joy in pain, punishment and following directions. Another was Jared who is rather fond of causing pain and letting me watch."

Weasel man turned around and gave me an eyebrow wiggle that made me want to barf.

Seriously, why are men so disgusting and *inclined to believe they are irresistible?*

Jared opened the door and stepped inside, Winnie and I following, with the final two entering the room and closing the door behind them. The three stood very close together and stared at me expectantly.

My eyes scanned the room. There was no décor or furniture. Instead of a guest house of dorms, wood shavings were laid on the floor with evenly spaced stalls. It didn't smell like animals live here, but I could hear sounds coming from somewhere. Every feature screamed newly built barn until I saw the red tinged wood in the low light of the southwest corner of the room. I sniffed but didn't smell redwood or popsicles.

"How many people have you killed here?" I guessed before looking at the identical smiles on all three faces. The first real sense of fear that my death would be slow and painful crept in.

"Irrelevant. Those who could not be brought about to my way of thinking were simply retired early in well-documented attacks on my safety. It's incredibly beneficial to start your collection with the lead agent, right Sarah?"

He caressed her cheek and she leaned into his touch.

"You killed people who were hired to protect you?" I felt anger burn my cheeks.

"No, I killed people who couldn't acknowledge when they've lost. I have delighted in converting my security detail into an entourage, but time is running out. My father has fallen ill and with his death certain truths will come to light that I promised to keep secret in exchange for a place here. While I cannot keep my father alive, nor can I un-do his provisions, I can find another bargaining chip to ensure my safety and continued prosperity here," he put his gun away and stroked both Sarah and Jared's cheeks. "Without my father to blame, your government will have to deal with me on where it is released or I will use it against them while sharing their secret with the world."

"What did your father do to become the scapegoat?" I asked, still piecing together how a virus and insurgents linked to a government cover-up and a son bearing false witness.

"He was there. The Americans declared his men insurgents, but they were there to give aid. When they saw what the Americans had done to those who were left... he wanted revenge. They eliminated the project and blamed him to cover up what he'd found. I corroborated that story and bought myself a place in the land of opportunity. No one thought he'd actually survived."

"And what did they do?" I asked, trying to decide if I should be scared or annoyed by his soliloquy. "What are you releasing?"

"They weaponized an aerosolized virus to encourage population control of the genetically undesirable. The agent attaches to genetic variations known to cause chronic and costly illnesses and mutates all of the neighboring coding regions until the body shuts down, contorted in agony. What was destroyed in those villages was not only the virus, but the remains of those unable to survive it. Did you really think only comic books speculated that humanity needed a check to its desire for unlimited replication?" He laughed dryly and I swallowed hard. "More than that, do you think the government would destroy its pet project and not keep anything for itself?"

My throat stuck together. Whoever had funded this, imagined it, was ahead of their time scientifically. Instead of helping the world, they tried to use science to create the perfect population. As though Nazi Germany wasn't who we'd fought against in World War Two.

"What do you need us for?" Winnie pressed her paw into my foot, acknowledging that she and I would get through this.

Together.

No matter how this ended, we would be together.

"I need you to find the last known sample of the virus. Its container utilizes minor explosives in the triggering of the distribution mechanism. The volume is about equal to the amount of gunpowder as you would find in a shotgun shell." He smiled down at Winnie and she showed him her pointiest teeth. "After my little test the other night, Winnie has proven herself more than capable. I was not prepared, however, for my father's men to intervene. I certainly wasn't expecting the betrayal you uncovered, but it has been rectified."

"That whole thing was a set-up to see if Winnie could find your explosive device? Why even have a party then? You could have just told Carla the favor you wanted was to see a bomb-sniffing dog in action and no one would have known you were bonkers until she found it!"

Conri tilted his head and Sarah delivered a roundhouse kick to my ribs that stole all the air from my lungs. Gasping, I gripped my ribs and tried to breathe through the agony.

"Do not insult me, Ms. Sharp. I will not tolerate disrespect. You will begin searching," he ordered, and I shook my head. Sarah delivered another kick and my body folded in on itself, sending me to the floor beside Winnie. "Search this facility, neighboring ones and find the tunnels or die."

"You ready girl?" I whispered quietly, letting my hair shield my mouth. The very tip of her tail wagged and I pressed a kiss to her snoot. "I love you, you're the best. On three?"

"What are you doing down there, Ms. Sharp?" A hand fisted in my hair and pulled me up from the ground, Jared's gun against my temple.

"Three!" I shouted and Winnie sprang forward, sinking her teeth into Sarah's arm at the same time that I kicked the heel of my boot into Jared's testicles. Gripping the wrist that was holding my hair, I spun under his arm and delivered two jabs to his ribs, stealing the gun from his hand and slamming it down on his head. Jared's body collapsed to the ground just as a cold metal barrel pressed against my cheek and I heard the hammer pull back on the gun.

"Enough!" Conri growled and I looked out of the corner of my eye. Winnie had Sarah on the ground, and the woman was screaming, but her gun was gone. Only two people were armed, and I had an advantage.

I didn't want anything from him and if he killed me, Winnie was useless.

"That is enough. You surrender and sit quietly until the cops get here," I ordered, and he let out a mirthless laugh. "Or whoever is coming."

"Why would I do that? You have no choice but to do what I say. I have a gun pointed at your head!" He mocked me but I shook my head against the gun.

"Doesn't matter. Kill me, don't kill me, you said yourself that you're out of time. What will you do if you kill me?"

"Use your dog to find the device and kill hundreds more," he shouted but I shook my head.

"You don't know how. She barely listened to the trainers at the Army, you really think she'd listen to you? Admit you've lost and no one needs to get hurt."

He turned suddenly and aimed the gun at Winnie. A decision that would not be tolerated and I fired two shots into his gut before slamming his body into the ground with Sarah beneath both of us. I nearly lost consciousness holding my breath against the deafening silence before I voiced my fear.

"Winnie?" I asked and felt her warm wet tongue on my cheek. I exhaled and held her close. "Now we have to do something bad."

She licked my face more and I climbed to my feet, checking the pulse of all three gunmen.

"I hope you and your father work things out in the afterlife," I whispered to a bleeding Conri before walking toward the door.

"Winnie, place," I commanded, pushing open the doors to the carriage house to see black ops guys running towards us with guns drawn. I raised my hands up, Winnie sitting and following suit in a "sit pretty" gesture of solidarity, waiting for them to surround us. "No matter what, we can't let them win. But you'll always be my favorite."

She wagged her tail in agreement and I let my knees fall to the ground while the nearest agent searched me.

Chapter Twenty-Five: One Last Time

"All rise," the bailiff called out and I quietly got to my feet. Behind me, I heard my parents stand while my nephew sobbed softly. Sylvia was on her best behavior and I delighted in the opportunity to give her a glimpse into her future if she didn't shape up.

The gentle clicking of her handheld video game let me know she was only quiet because my mom distracted her. The girl would learn nothing from this experience... kind of like me.

It's sad when poor decision making is the only discernible family trait that continued for generations.

A judge in black robes sat down, the rest of the panel following suit but I remained standing until granted permission. The people seated around the judge were solemn-faced. Some in military uniforms, some in traditional suits, and none of them felt inclined to speak to me and identify their name or allegiance.

This court session was closed to the public and aside from my family, friends and those who were present at the time of Conri's capture, there was no one to witness my fate and I was grateful. I would go quietly if they arrested me, but I wouldn't let them take Winnie.

If they reached for her fluffy neck, I would rain hellfire down upon the courthouse.

Or... Winnie farts.

I still wasn't permitted near explosives.

"Please be seated," the bailiff called, looking at me with something that resembled pity.

I didn't need pity.

This whole trial was a waste of effort and energy, since the world knew what the American government had done. Winnie and I had returned to the Taft property in the middle of the night, located the device and disposed of it in a secured tunnel. We then used tactically acquired explosives Winnie located in the bunker of an easily accessed "secure" military base and then collapsed the tunnel on itself.

The bunker's ownership by the Department of Homeland Security was another reason we were here today. It was not very tactical to acquire it on camera with a mocking jab at the lack of security used by the Department of Homeland *Security*.

References may have been made to TSA and government effectiveness.

The incident was filmed and submitted to the national media, sparking Conri's father to release his files and documents. There was an uproar, protests, and demands that the creators of such a weapon be publicly hanged only to find that those involved were already dead. Not even the science could be deemed valuable with the evolution of genetic sequencing and interpretation. Aside from the remains of those murdered overseas being located and laid to rest, there was nothing to gain from exposing them.

With no one to punish, the public forgot and I was placed under house arrest for violation of an executive order of confidentiality and theft of government property. In my mind, I knew I had done the right thing. There was no one on earth I trusted with an aerosolized virus and I could live with my decision if it meant I never had to wonder where it was.

It was also thrilling to steal explosives from the government with my best friend.

Then detonate them.

My life was recently lacking in opportunities to detonate explosives.

The restrictions that came with my initial hearing allowed me to work at the dairy, purchase groceries and visit my parents. Instead of an ankle monitor, a GPS device was inserted beneath the skin of my lower back. The device used cell phones, cell towers and smart watches to ping my location. Aside from being itchy and impossible to misplace, there was no real difference between having this chip and carrying a cell phone. It had been a month, but they were finally ready to sentence me and I couldn't help the knot sitting heavily in my stomach.

Winnie popped her head up beside me at the table and I stroked her ears. She'd also been ordered here today, a reminder that she was a privilege of my honorable discharge and they could take her away. The real privilege would be watching whoever tried taking her away find out exactly how much cheese it took for a lactose-intolerant dog to take out a courthouse.

Because I had not held back this morning in preparation for my appearance.

"Ms. Sharp?" The judge spoke and I stood up at my table, ready for whatever they threw at me. While they were monitoring me, I was making plans of my own. What they decided could not hurt Winnie as Ian Cruz had shared just enough information to take care of any ties Winnie had to the Army. Ties that unfortunately meant he got a slap on the wrist in the form of a suspension, but thanks to him, there would be no legal record of Winnie belonging to the Army.

Well, him and Mrs. Margot's "cracker" who offered the military an anonymous and very critical review of their records' security system. It rivaled my review of their physical security on explosives storage containers, but was far more eloquent and contained fewer references to the movie *Stripes*. Unfortunately for them, she placed it in a secure folder labeled "Open Me" but no one remembered the password.

The password had been 'password' and none of the de-encryption programs could guess that.

"Yes, your Honor ?" I spoke when she paused longer than I found comfortable and she looked at me over the top of half-moon spectacles.

"You have been under GPS monitoring for a month, as well as audio and video surveillance. Are you aware of the reasoning for this precautionary measure?"

"Yes, your Honor ," I answered her and she looked down at the paper in front of her.

"Do you know what these observations concluded, Ms. Sharp?"

"No, your Honor ," I said, feeling a heavy feeling settle on my shoulders. In the past two months I'd been impaled on a tree, publicly assaulted with a riding crop, scalped by a cat and shoved from a moving car by my niece. While it had felt like a perfectly normal month to me, I hadn't a clue what the court's interpretation of those events would be. Winnie had similarly caused a scene at a grocery store over lunch meat, dumped two gallons of pasteurized milk and peed on a visiting presidential candidate.

If their conclusion was that we were both a hazardous menace to society, our single argument would be that most of the hazard was to ourselves. Society would likely just feel bereft of enter-tainment if we were removed from it.

"Ms. Sharp, you and that dog are national heroes. You have served your country with fidelity, that often lacked decorum and respectability, but no one here believes you are a threat to na-tional security nor to the population as a whole beyond yourself. Weapons theft aside, we would like to express our approval that you detonated them on government property with complete accountability as to the resources utilized and regard shown to public safety."

I felt my mom inhale sharply behind me and I couldn't help the laugh that bubbled out of my throat.

For the second time in my life, a judge facing me smiled and it wasn't because I had dog crap stuck to my shoe.

"Unfortunately, you ignored an executive order, caused civil unrest, and accessed munitions without written authorization."

I felt my laughter run away. No good deed would make them forget I hadn't followed orders... again. As though they didn't know it was what I would do, especially after I filed the necessary paperwork.

Granted the paperwork was un-signed, unofficial and contained a few too many pictographs of lewd hand gestures to ever be permissible in an administrative record.

Still, I at least filled it out.

"As a result, you are sentenced to one year of community service at the VA Hospital in Dayton. You are asked to bring your dog and spend time with the veterans who have suffered serious or traumatic injury and offer comfort and support to them and their family. You are required to do 8 hours a week for one year. At the completion of this service, your tracker will be removed."

My smile returned.

This wasn't a punishment, it was an opportunity and I couldn't let go of the feeling that I would once again be able to help people.

With live entertainment and dog kisses.

"All other restrictions are lifted. You and Sgt. Pupperson are free to go," she closed the file in front of her and everyone stood. "Ms. Sharp, you did the right thing. Even if no one wants to acknowledge it, the country is safer for what you have done."

She and the remaining council members exited and the bailiff held open the wooden gate to the galley where my family was waiting with Cruz, Stella, James and Daniel Kirby. Though no one was standing too close to the last and were eyeing him like a stranger in a white panel van.

"What brings you here, deputy?" I asked and everyone became quiet waiting for the answer.

"I came to see them throw the book at you, but I guess they ran out of books," he scoffed before pulling me in for a hug. "I'm also here because Larry wouldn't come but I know he'd be pissed if he found out something bad happened to you from someone who wasn't here. I hope you two work it out, I'd like to have you as a sister in law."

My mom and Carla said *aww* while Cruz pretended he hadn't heard. I reached back and took his hand, pulling him close. Whatever he and I were, his efforts to keep me safe and united with Winnie was enough for me. I wanted him and for now I had him.

It was enough.

"Thank you, for your help," I said, referencing his efforts to reunite the now legal Canadians with their families and keeping Mrs. Margot's niece from being arrested. He also inadvertently introduced "the cracker" to one of those Canadians and apparently her aunt's sloppy seconds were "no big" because Daniel's cousin moved in with her two days ago.

He's learning coding and other IT skills so he can work with something besides his body.

"Yeah, well, their families aren't saying that. Apparently those old ladies spoiled them and now they don't know how to act like grown-ups." I snickered at the audacity of the person saying it and gestured up and down his frame. "Ha freaking ha, you know what I mean."

Daniel shook my hand before he walked back up the aisle, my mom, brother and sister Heidi following him while my niece and nephew were stampeding out of the court playing fighter plane. Carla linked her arm with me on the opposite side of where Cruz was standing, the grim expression she'd worn the past month finally fading with the outcome of the trial.

"Next time, include me will you? I have connections, I could have... I don't know... Kept you from this?" She said and I smiled with a head shake. We'd had this conversation so many times I couldn't help but feel irked that she thought I would jeopardize her or my brother's kids by letting her get involved in my shenanigans.

"Plausible deniability. Besides, this was hardly a punishment. If I'd known you could volunteer at a VA hospital I'd probably already be doing it." She laughed, giving me a tight hug.

"That's fair. Try to leave the hospital standing and without needing them to treat you for injuries every week, OK?" She joked, leaving me standing with Cruz just outside the courthouse.

"No promises!" I shouted after her and she responded with a finger wave over her shoulder.

"So, now what?" I asked Cruz, Winnie sitting between us with her head on my leg. "Kind of regretting all the cheese I gave her now..."

"Well, I have protection at my house and we didn't get around to testing the couch yet. It has a sixty day warranty that could end any day now." He wiggled his eyebrows and I smiled.

"Only if there's coffee."

"For you, chica, there's always coffee," he took my hand, kissing the palm before linking our fingers and heading back to his house. "Coffee and dogs. I know how to keep my women happy."

He definitely does, I thought, leaning back to admire his butt.

"Well then... let's go test the tensile strength of your couch, Sgt. Hottie," I smiled and gave him a wink. He turned to the side, trapping my arms and kissing me hard.

"Maybe we should check the beds again, too. Just in case... and the kitchen counters... maybe also the..."

I kissed him to stop the suggestions. My body was already more than excited to get going on his plans. Grabbing his hand, I started pulling him to the car faster, Winnie at our heels.

"Thank dog I didn't wear underwear today."

Autumn In the Woods with Dogs

Traveling through the
carnage,

Beautiful death, bursting
with color.

The fiery foliage con-
suming the light,

A mystery to mull over.

E. N. CRANE

With every step, the
leaves crunch,

An auditory reminder
of their demise.

But one pawed creature
pounces in delight,

I try to see autumn
through their eyes.

The crisp air refreshing,
a welcome relief.

Prancing on toes that
caress the ground.

With the wind in their
fur and freedom to run,

Their joy mingling with
the breeze the only
sound.

It's past midday, a time
for rest.

Yet trekking the path,
there is no fatigue.

Only beautiful shimmers
and patches of shade.

Only a sense we've finally
been freed.

Our feet pound the earth,
senses alight.

The path growing nar-
row, winding through
trees.

A brilliant lake keeping
us on course,

A compass that ebbs and
flows as it pleases.

At the end of the line, we
start to head back.

Our heads and hearts
lighter,

There is no greater peace.

Then spending a day
with my dogs in the trees.

*Two dogs on a trail
with fall foliage behind
them*

About the Author

E. N. Crane is a fiction author writing humorous mysteries with plus-sized female leads and their furry friends. She is one of two authors under the Perry Dog Publishing Imprint, a one woman, two dog operation in Idaho... for now. My dogs are Perry and Padfoot, the furry beasts shown above. They are well-loved character inspiration in all things written and business.

If you are interested in joining my newsletter, please subscribe here: https://e-n-crane_perrydogpublishing.ck.page/578ed9ab 37or on my website, PerryDogPublishing.com

You will receive A Bite in Afghanistan, the prequel to the Sharp Investigations Series, as a thank-you for joining. I only have one newsletter for mental health reasons, so both romance and mystery are on there! If you only want one in your inbox, follow

Perry Dog Publishing on all socials to stay on top of the latest news... and pet pics.

Made in the USA
Las Vegas, NV
10 December 2024

13816955R00155